GAMES

GAMES

CAROL GORMAN

HarperCollins*Publishers*

Library of Congress Cataloging-in-Publication Data is available.
ISBN-10: 0-06-057027-X (trade bdg.) — ISBN-13: 978-0-06-057027-9 (trade bdg.)
ISBN-10: 0-06-057028-8 (lib. bdg.) — ISBN-13: 978-0-06-057028-6 (lib. bdg.)

Typography by Larissa Lawrynenko
1 2 3 4 5 6 7 8 9 10

First Edition

To Linda Gregan Northcutt,
educator *extraordinaire*, Sioux City, Iowa,
who mentioned that when two students at
her school were caught fighting, she
required them to play games until they
could figure out how to get along.

I would like to thank Mary Carson and her granddaughter, Chelsea Hines, for their help and for telling me about peaches in shoes.

CHAPTER ONE

Boot's Turn

I WALK DOWN THE HALL before school starts and nod at the Water Street kids. They say, "hey," or nod back, like we're brothers. I hardly look at the jocks or the pretty boys. I'm a ghost to them, invisible—they don't even know I'm here. Everybody's opening their lockers and slamming them shut.

"Hey, Boot!" a voice calls out. I turn to see Jerrod Kitchen standing at his locker. "We got a game after school," J.K. says. (All the Water Street kids call him by his initials.) "Meet at the Corner."

I hold up my hand to tell him I'll be there. That's when I see Mick Sullivan coming down the hall. He's watching me, and he's got this big smile on his face that says he thinks he's better than everybody else. That smile alone makes me want to smash him. He's a big kid, built like a road grader. He plants himself right in front of me so I have to look up to see him, and he grins down at my face. "Hi, Boot, you lunatic. You've been on my mind. . . . You want to know why?"

"No," I say.

People stop to watch. Some are my friends—kids from Water Street. They have big, staring eyes and kind of a bloodthirsty look. They expect me to throw the first punch as usual. Even though he's got thirty pounds on me, I'm not scared.

He goes, "It's because I realized last night who you remind me of: Yosemite Sam. You know, that guy in the Bugs Bunny cartoons with the cowboy clothes and the long mustache? He's got a very bad temper, and he's always shooting off his guns the way you shoot off your mouth."

I hear a few snickers around me.

"I think I'll start calling you 'Yosemite.' How do ya like that?"

More snickers.

I'm tired because I didn't get much sleep last night, so I don't punch him, even though he deserves it. Instead of hitting him, I look up his nostrils and say, "You got a booger up there."

Everybody laughs loud now, so on the scorecard in my head, I give myself a point.

Mick takes a step back and laughs. "That's it?" He holds out his hands, palms up. "That's all ya *got*?" He laughs again. "I expected you to take a punch or at least insult me."

2

"He said you got a booger up your nose, Sullivan," J.K. says. I realize now he's standing behind me. "Seems like an insult to me."

"Yeah." But I say it a second or two too late, so I sound like a little kid who's letting his big brother do the talking.

Mick goes, "That's no insult. You should've said something *really* insulting like . . ." He stares over my head and squints like he's thinking real hard. "Hmm, something like, *'I once scraped something off the bottom of my shoe that looked like you.'* Or wait, here's another one: *'You look familiar—oh, no, I was thinking about something I baited my hook with once.'* That wasn't too bad. Or you could even have said, *'Hey, is that your face, or did your neck throw up?'*"

Even my friends laugh at that one. I suddenly feel hot, and my armpits are sweating.

Mick grins down at me. "That last one is especially funny, if I do say so myself."

"How about this one?" I ask him. "'I hear your dad was thrown in the slammer for drunk driving again. He might as well be lying in a gutter somewhere with the rest of the garbage.'"

That gets him like I thought it would. He freezes a second, then lunges at me, and knocks me over. He gets down and starts slugging me in the stomach. Mick isn't tough, but he's big, and he's really mad, so he doesn't pull his punches. I don't feel the pain now—that'll come later. Right now I'm thinking about holding my own. I get in some good licks before Mr. Jefferson hauls Mick up by his collar to a standing position.

"That's it, Sullivan," he yells in Mick's face. "You, too, Quinn," he hollers at me as I get to my feet. "What's the *matter* with you boys? Didn't your last suspensions teach you *anything*?" He grabs my arm in a steel-vise grip and marches us down the hall toward the principal's office. Everyone turns to watch; some look disgusted, but a few of my friends hold their fists up in kind of a salute to me.

Mr. Jefferson doesn't let go till we're in the main office. He points at two chairs. "Sit. And no talking." He leans over and says something I can't hear to Mrs. Taylor, the principal's secretary. She nods and shoots us a mean look. He walks into the principal's office. I don't hear too good out of my left ear, so I turn to point my right ear in the direction of the office. I figure he's talking to the principal. His name is Mr. Block, but most of us call him Blockhead. Not to his face, though.

Then I remember. Mr. Block had a heart attack. I heard the teachers say it was because of all the years of putting up with the rotten kids at this school, but they're wrong. He didn't put up with us at all. He was always suspending people for a week. Two weeks ago it was me. And Mick Sullivan.

Mick sits on the chair across from me. I don't look at him. I'm sick and tired of how he's always in my face, acting like he's better than me. I knew calling his old man a piece of garbage would make him mad, but I didn't make up the part about the drunk driving. I heard it from three people.

Mr. Jefferson comes out of the principal's office and gestures for Mick and me to come. We get up and walk behind the counter and into Blockhead's office.

A new guy is there. He gets up from his desk, and I swear he looks like he could win a tug-of-war with a cement truck. I start to sweat.

He says thanks to Mr. Jefferson, who scowls at us for good measure, and goes out.

The principal says "Sit down," in this big voice, so we don't argue. We sit in these plastic chairs. He comes around the desk. He's big as a mountain. "Mick and . . ." He frowns at a piece of paper in his hand. "Which one of you is Boot?"

"My real name is Bart," I say in this little voice, "but I go by Boot." I don't say any more than I have to. I hope he doesn't ask me how I got the name. People started calling me Bart Simpson and saying things like, "Hey, Bart, does your dad go, 'D'oh!' all the time?" and I got pretty sick of it. So a few years ago, I told the Water Street guys to call me Boot, and by the time I started middle school, everybody called me that. But the principal might not like that. Or he might start calling me Bart just to show me he can.

So I'm surprised when he nods and goes, "All right, Boot." Then he turns to both of us. "I'm Mr. Maddox, your new principal."

I usually stare at the floor in the principal's office and

count the linoleum tiles while I'm getting yelled at. (There's half a tile between the desk and the wall, and fifteen tiles from the front of his desk to the wall at the end of the room.) But this time I stare at the principal. He's not yelling yet, but he's so big, I want to keep an eye on him. Then he does something that's pretty unheard of. He puts out his hand for me to shake. At first, I'm not sure that's what he means—I mean, I've never heard of a principal doing that before, so it takes a second for me to realize that's why his huge, beefy hand is hanging there in front of me.

I give him my hand, and he shakes it. He doesn't crush the bones, but I know he could if he wanted to.

He turns and says, "Mick?" Mick jabs his fat hand at the guy, and they shake. Mick smiles like maybe he's hoping the principal will like him because he's big, too.

"I understand that you young men have a history of fighting. Is that right?"

Silence. Now I look at the floor, but I hear him say, "I don't know you yet, so I want to make sure I'm getting accurate information."

That surprises me. He isn't just going to take Mr. Jefferson's say-so.

"Yeah," Mick says. "It's fair to say we have a history of fighting."

"Okay," he says. "Is it true that this is the second fight this year?"

"Well, actually," Mick says, looking up at him, "it's the fifth or sixth, but only the second at school."

I look over at Mick now, and he's smiling, trying to get on his good side. He's hoping that the principal will like him better than me.

"Thanks for your honesty," the guy says, and he looks over at a calendar on the wall. "But you've had two fights since school started, and it's only September eighth. That must be a record."

I know it's not a record. My brother got into so many fights, he was kicked out of middle school for the last three months of eighth grade. But I don't say so.

"I want to know what happened out there, and I want to hear from both of you. Mick, why don't you go first?"

Mick glances at me, then back at the guy. "Okay. Well, I was walking down the hall and saw Boot, who's this really crabby guy. He's got a bad temper, and when he's mad you can hear him a block away. So I told him he reminds me of Yosemite Sam—from the cartoons. He didn't say anything, and I wondered if he knew who Yosemite *is*. So I told him that he's this guy with a long mustache, right? Who's always getting mad and shooting off his guns. Then he said some really insulting things, so I took a punch at him." He shrugs. "That's what was going on when Mr. Jefferson came along."

The principal looks at me now. "Is that what happened?"

"He forgot to tell what I said to him first," I say. To tell you the truth, I think my booger comment was pretty funny, so I want it on the record.

"And what was that?" he asks.

"I said he had a booger in his nose." I glance at Mick, but he isn't reacting. He just sits there.

"Okay," the guy says. He doesn't smile, so I wonder if he's pretending the joke isn't funny, or if he just doesn't have a sense of humor. With a principal, you never know. "Then what?"

"Well, then he laughs and says I should've hit him or said something really insulting. He gives me this list of things I could've said."

"Really?" He looks kind of surprised.

"Yeah," I say. "So I insulted him back."

"What did you say?"

Then I realize I should've kept my mouth shut. Now I have to tell what I said to Sullivan. I glance over at him, and he has this little smile on his face and his eyebrows go up, like he planned all along for me to tell this part.

I shift in my chair and scratch my head even though it doesn't itch. I stare at the floor. I say kind of quiet, "Well . . . I said I heard about his dad getting picked up for drunk driving." I look up and rush to say the next part. "But he was calling me names."

Mr. Maddox nods. "You probably knew that saying that about his dad would make him pretty mad."

I look at the floor again. The linoleum's kind of chipped in this one spot, and the part that's missing looks like a guy's face that has a broken nose.

"Most of us are protective about our families," he says. He looks at Mick. "And calling Boot names made him mad enough to insult your dad. You want to say anything to Boot now?"

I glance up at Mick. He's looking at me and goes, "I guess I could apologize, but he'll have to say it first. What he said about my dad was a lot worse than me telling him he reminds me of Yosemite Sam."

"What do you have to say about that, Boot?" he asks.

I have the feeling that if I don't just say it, I'll wish I had. And even though the principal is big, he doesn't seem all that scary. So I say, "I'm not sorry. He's always in my face, trying to make me look stupid."

I glare up at Mick, realizing I just handed him an opening to say something like, "I don't have to *try* to do that." I've heard things like that from him since fourth grade. Anyway, that's what he's thinking, too, because he smiles and lifts his eyebrows at me again. But he doesn't want to lose the points he just scored with the principal, so he doesn't say what he's thinking.

A few more seconds go by, and then the guy walks over to the doorway of a room just off his office. He stands there with his back to us, and he pretty much fills up the whole doorway. He says, "You young men need to learn how to get along with each other."

After another second or two, he turns around to face us. "I'd like you two to come here tomorrow and maybe for a few days after that. You'll spend some time in this room and play games."

I frown. Play *games*? I wonder if I heard right. I look over at Mick who looks like he can't believe it, either. His mouth is hanging open, and he looks really stupid.

The principal must be a mind reader because he says, "That's right. I want you to play games. I'll talk with your teachers and your parents and explain what we're doing. We'll start at eleven o'clock tomorrow. You'll play board games for an hour, walk down to get your lunches, and then you'll come back here to eat and play some more." He looks back and forth at us. "Got it?"

Mick says, "Got it." But he says it like he thinks it's a bad idea.

"Boot?" he says to me.

I scowl at Mick. I want him to know he better watch out. "Yeah," I say.

I hope Mick can read minds. Because the first chance I get, inside or out of school, I'm going to flatten his face.

CHAPTER TWO

Mick's Turn

I CAN'T HELP IT. When the opportunity is there—Boot standing in the hallway, right out in the open—I can't stop myself. It's like waving a tenderloin under the nose of a starving man. It's not that I just *want* to irritate him. It's more like I *have* to. He looks so funny when his eyes narrow to little slits, and he bares his teeth at me. I expect him to haul out his six-shooters and blast away like Yosemite Sam, hollering, "You gol durn varmint!"

Don't get me wrong, I'm not a tough guy. (My dad will attest to that.) I don't like fighting. That's just the price I have to pay for the pleasure of tormenting Boot Quinn. Sometimes provoking Boot to start a fight is the most interesting thing that happens all day.

But he went too far, insulting my dad. I won't lie; my dad

11

drinks a lot. I'd even say he's an alcoholic. But he's *my* alcoholic, and nobody's going to talk about him like that.

Anyway, after Mr. Maddox hands down our sentence, Boot and I walk into the hallway. I expect that he'll give us a stern warning or walk out into the corridor to make sure we don't start punching each other again. But he doesn't do either, and we're left standing in the hall by ourselves.

"How come you always come to school with wet hair?" I ask him.

Boot looks mad. He turns away and mumbles something.

"You're going to have to speak up," I tell him. "In fact, try yelling; you're pretty good at that."

Boot's eyes go down to slits, and he says, "I'm gonna come after you, Sullivan. Maybe not at school, but real soon I'm gonna wipe the floor with you."

"I'm a little big for that, Boot," I say. "I don't think you could drag me more than an inch or two. And this is a pretty big floor to wipe. But maybe you meant that metaphorically."

I'm not exaggerating when I say he's funny when he's mad. It's like he's a bad actor, and he's overacting, really chewing scenery. His face gets a fiery red, he clenches his fists till his fingers turn white, and I swear you can almost see arrows shooting out of his eyes. It's hilarious.

"You just wait," he growls and heads down to the other end of the building.

I shrug and watch him go. "Okay, Boot," I say cheerfully to his shrinking back as he walks away down the hall. "See you tomorrow at eleven."

I go to my first-period class. But I'm thinking this sentence playing games might not be so bad.

Two years ago, at the beginning of sixth grade, Boot and I were in the same language arts class. This was before the people at school figured out they'd better separate us. Our teacher, Ms. Murphy, assigned us to the same group to work on a report and panel discussion. Boot sat back, as usual, not doing anything, staring off into space, while Sarah Lisinski, Jenny Barker, and I did all the work. Sarah and Jenny are good students, so it wasn't as if the whole burden was on me. But it ticked me off to see Boot doing his tree stump imitation—a skinny little tree stump, but no more animated—while the three of us researched the topic, which was the life and work of William Carlos Williams, this poet we were reading. Boot would get the same grade we got.

I suggested to Sarah and Jenny that we work on the report at school and organize our panel discussion at one of our houses. I knew that Boot wouldn't ask why we weren't working on the panel discussion, and he didn't. He probably didn't pay attention enough to know we were *supposed* to organize a panel discussion. But because I didn't want to feel even a shred of guilt later, I told him that we were going to work on it after school at Jenny's house, and I even gave him the address. He shrugged—didn't ask any questions—and of course, he didn't show up. So we figured it was fair to go on without him.

The day our group was to present our report, the four of us sat at a long table in front of the class. Sarah, Jenny, and I talked about Williams's life, told everyone that he was also a doctor who took care of middle-class and poor people in New Jersey, and then we read some of his poems and talked about them.

Boot just sat in his chair at the table with us and glowered. The kids in class watched him, and some were trying not to laugh, as it became more obvious that he wasn't going to open his mouth.

At the end of our presentation, Ms. Murphy asked Boot if he had anything to add. He scowled and said no.

So I told her that Boot isn't a joiner; he meanders to a different drummer.

Some of the kids cracked up. Ms. Murphy flashed a smile, and then realized she shouldn't encourage me and wiped the smile off her face. After language arts class, Boot tackled me in the hallway, and I mean that literally. That christened our present career as middle-school enemies. Three fights and three suspensions later—by second semester—it was clear that we wouldn't be put in any more classes together.

I've seen the inside of the principal's office many times. But the new principal, Mr. Maddox, was a surprise, and in more ways than one. First, he's built like a fullback, with a deep, resonant voice. I'd have guessed that he'd use his size and voice to his advantage. You know, to intimidate the two kids in his office.

But he didn't. He *shook our hands.* Man, I wasn't expecting anything friendly. Then he told us that our punishment for fighting is *playing games* every day, and I wondered where they found this guy. But, hey, if he wants Boot and me to play games as a punishment, I'll sacrifice and do it.

Rumor has it that Boot's classes are scheduled at one end of the school and mine at the other, making it less likely we'll run into each other. Of course, that doesn't help. Sometimes, to relieve the boredom, I go looking for him. It's fun—and cheap entertainment—and I take that wherever I can get it.

Most people think my favorite class would be P.E. because of my size. The football coach cornered me on the first day of middle school and asked if I'd like to join the team. I said, "No thanks," but he kept trying to persuade me. I knew that after he saw me blunder through gym class, he'd quickly change his mind. I might be big, but I'm no jock. I don't run; I lumber. I don't jump; I lurch. I don't play sports; I lie on the couch and read. In short, I'm a klutz, a wuss. Just ask my dad.

I tried to tell the coach that I wasn't football-star material, but he called my home and asked to talk to my dad. I handed the phone to him and then hung around the living room, so I could hear his side of the conversation.

"Yes, coach," he said. "I think Mick should play football, too. He's sure got his size going for him. But I'm sorry to say he's not interested in sports. Sometimes I wonder if I got the wrong kid at the hospital." He let out this nervous laugh.

Dad's usually a nice guy when he's not drinking, and at that time, he'd been on the wagon for almost two months. Mom and I were watching him carefully, because two months is a long time for him to go without drinking. We were hoping that this time it would stick.

He finally hung up the phone and turned to me. "Coach says the team could use you."

"I'd be an embarrassment to the team," I said. "You know that."

"I don't know that," my dad answered. There was an irritated edge to his voice. "You haven't tried."

Adrenaline was beginning to shoot through my body. That's for fight or flight, and I was thinking flight sounded like the better plan—my dad's a lot bigger than Boot. I was pretty sure Dad wouldn't shove me around, though. He only does that sometimes when he's been drinking.

"Dad," I said, trying to sound reasonable and mature while trying to swallow my spleen which had just leaped into my throat. "I wouldn't want to embarrass myself, or you, or the school. So let's not talk about it, okay?"

He shook his head. "Okay, boy," he said. "I see I'm wasting my time. But you're making a big mistake. You could have talent you don't even know about."

I thought I'd leave it at that and went to my room. I was glad he didn't bring up the subject again—at least not then. Not until about a week later when he fell off the wagon. But that's another story.

CHAPTER THREE

Boot's Turn

I WALK AWAY FROM Mick, who's still standing in the middle of the hallway. "See you tomorrow at eleven," he says. He makes his voice fake-friendly, like we're buddies meeting later for a ball game or something. I don't turn around but keep walking. I'm itching to yell some bad words at him, but I just yell them in my head because I don't want to go back to the principal's office.

That new principal is weird. I figured he'd give us another suspension like Mr. Block always did. He'd yell about "zero tolerance," and tell us he was kicking us out of school for two days. Then he'd call my dad, who thought Block was a jerk because he was always calling about my brother, Ethan.

Anyway, I never heard of a principal who makes enemies stay in the same room on purpose. And play games. Maybe he's never been a principal before and doesn't know any better. Maybe he'll see what middle school is really like and get mean by next week. I make a bet with myself that he'll start threatening people before a month is over. All he'd have to do is look mean, and anybody with a brain would shape up. He looks like he could do a lot of damage if he wanted to.

I wonder what it'll be like tomorrow. I can hardly stand to look at Sullivan, so how am I supposed to play games with him? I get kind of nervous thinking about it, and that makes me mad. Mick doesn't scare me, but he always acts like he's so much smarter and better than me. If I make any stupid mistakes—and that might happen because I can be pretty dumb sometimes—I know he'll laugh and tell everybody that he used to just *think* I was an idiot. Now I've *proved* it. He loves saying stuff like that. I wonder if I can be in the same room with Sullivan for a whole hour, plus lunch, and not knock his head off.

I get to my science class. Ms. White's talking, but she stops and looks at the pass I got from the principal's office. J.K. sits at the side of the room by the fish tank; he laughs when he sees me.

"Hey, Quinn," he says loud enough for everyone to hear. "How come you're not suspended?" He glances up at the teacher to see how she's reacting, but she's gone to the door to cross my name off the absent slip. J.K. looks around the room at Scott Berkey and Clay Sizemore, who laugh. Berkey and Sizemore live a block from Water Street. We've been friends as long as I can remember.

I give J.K. a thumbs-up. "New principal," I say. "No problem. I got it handled."

"New principal?" Berkey says, swiveling in his seat to talk to me. "What's his name?"

"I don't know. Something."

Ms. White pretends she doesn't hear anything going on in her classroom and starts talking again. Something about rocks. I'm not too interested in rocks—in fact, I'm pretty bored with the whole subject of rocks, to tell you the truth—so I slide down in my seat and think about other stuff.

One of the major things I think about is music, because I want to play in a band. My friend Jesse says most rock musicians start playing guitar about my age, so I figure I can do it, too. Jesse plays in Otis Wants Bread, a band that's getting pretty known around here. Bruce Springsteen's his hero, even though he's pretty old—and Jesse says he's a classic. Jesse's band is working on a CD and planning a tour for next summer, and I bet they hit it big soon after that. It'd be so cool to say I knew him when. . . . Then I could get famous, too, and Jesse and I could maybe tour in the same band.

Jesse's my best friend, even though he's seventeen. I met him one night last summer when I heard rock music pouring out of his dad's store. You could feel the bass vibrating across the street. The door was open to let in some air, so I hung out in the doorway until he noticed me, and we started talking. Jesse waits on customers at River City Music and tells them about all the guitars and amps and stuff.

After hours, he plays. He knows more about guitars than just about anybody. I look through catalogs and pick out the guitars I'm going to buy someday. I've got my eye on a Gibson Les Paul Standard, which would feel real cool in my hands and Jesse says would wail like nothing you ever heard. But maybe someday I'll be so rich, I can get a Custom Shop '59.

So like I said, Jesse likes Springsteen's music more than any other. Jesse says the way he plays guitar makes him think he's sending up smoke signals, there's so much he's saying along with the chords and stuff.

I like to listen to the CDs by Otis Wants Bread and think about how cool it would be to travel all over the country— maybe even the world—and play hard-driving rock all the time with Jesse and the guys.

Tabitha Slater, who sits ahead of me one row over, turns around and shoots a rubber band. It *thwaps* me in the forehead and flops onto my desk. I look over at her. She smiles and covers her mouth with her hand.

If it had been any other person, I'd have gotten mad. But Tabitha's too cute to get mad at. A lot of the guys are hung up on her, even though they think she's out of their league. She has this wavy blonde hair that she's always flipping over her shoulder and a great laugh. I could listen to her laugh all day. She takes her hand away and smiles wider, showing the braces on her teeth.

I can feel my face getting hot, but I shoot the rubber band back at her. She lets out this squeal and turns away, so it won't hit her face. The rubber band hits her arm, and she grabs for it, but it falls on the floor.

"Boot, would you like to take another trip to the principal's office?" Ms. White asks.

Tabitha's laughing now, along with some other people. For a second, I try to keep a smile off my face, but a laugh explodes from my mouth. Everybody laughs harder.

"Well?" Ms. White says.

I get hold of myself and go, "No, I guess not." But now I don't mind that I can't keep from smiling.

"Tabitha, turn around," says Ms. White. She sounds mad.

Tabitha turns toward the front, but I can see her shoulders shaking, so I know she's still laughing.

We all quiet down, and I pretend to listen to Ms. White, but I sit there and think about Tabitha, who is a whole lot more interesting than any rocks you could talk about. So even though I got in trouble, the day doesn't end up being all that bad.

After school, I meet J.K. at his locker. "Where's the game?" I ask.

"At the vacant lot. We're meeting Clay and Matt at the Corner."

"You bring the football?" I ask.

"Yeah." He gets it from the bottom of his locker.

We don't exactly play football with rules and stuff. We just get a bunch of guys together to throw the ball around. The vacant lot is about three blocks from school.

Me and J.K. go outside and start walking to the Corner Market. It's a convenience store at the corner of Highland and Crescent, a block from school, where kids go for sodas and stuff to eat.

"So what happened with the new principal?" J.K. asks me.

"Not much," I say. "At least till tomorrow."

"Yeah? So then what?"

"I gotta play games with Sullivan."

"What do you mean, you gotta *play games*?" he says.

"I guess like Monopoly and stuff. Maybe cards. He says we gotta play games for an hour—plus lunch—till we can get along. It's stupid. I'll never get along with Sullivan, no matter how long we have to play games. I hate him."

J.K.'s laugh sounds like a snort. "The principal likes dog fighting, too? Put two dogs in a pen and watch 'em fight till one is dead? 'Cause that's what's going to happen with you and Sullivan. Where you gonna play these games?"

"I don't know. Somewhere."

"Man, that guy's gotta be crazy," J.K. says. Then he smiles. "I wish I could watch. I'd take bets on how long it would take for you to kill each other."

"He better not try and mess with me," I say. Just thinking about getting trapped in a room with Sullivan for an hour and a half sends heat and anger shooting through me. I feel like tracking him down right now.

Clay Sizemore and Matt Thumm are at the Corner when we get there. They're eating ice cream and looking over a big Harley parked outside.

"Man, look at those ape hangers," I say, grabbing one of the high handlebars. "This is a Springer."

"What's that?" Matt asks.

I show him the springs and shocks on the front end. "Harley made this model like seventy years ago, and then in the sixties, and they brought 'em back again. I saw one in my brother's Harley catalog."

"It's so cool," Clay says. I can tell he's impressed.

J.K. smacks me on the arm and nods toward the street. "Hey, Boot, here comes your games guy."

Clay and Matt say, "Hunh?" and we all look over to see Mick Sullivan walking in our direction.

"Come on," I say. I'm feeling more like fighting now than I did at school. I hear J.K. say, "Yeah." Clay and Matt are right there with me. They follow me to the middle of the sidewalk, and we stand together and block his way.

I can see him take in a breath, and he looks kind of scared because there are four of us.

"Look who's here," I say. He stops in front of us. He tries to put a smirk on his face, but it slides off, and I can tell he's pretty worried. I'm feeling better and better. I hope he starts to sweat real bad. I give him a surprised look. "Aren't you going to say hello, Sullivan?"

He glances around at the four of us. "H'lo," he says.

"I think he looks scared," I say.

"Yeah," J.K. says. Clay and Matt laugh. "You scared, Sullivan?"

Mick takes a breath and lets it out. "No," he says. "I'm just terribly alert." But I can tell he's trying to keep himself calm. "Okay, I'm scared. Very scared, in fact. You've got four, and I'm only one."

"Hey, you're right, Mickey," I say and laugh. "There are *four* of us and only one of you. I think we should squash you into a little grease spot on the sidewalk." My friends laugh. "Well," I say, looking him up and down, "maybe a big grease spot." Now they really laugh.

But I'm suspicious. *Why would Sullivan admit he's scared?* I figure he's got something up his sleeve.

J.K. smiles, and says, "If he's so scared, maybe he'd like to make a run for it."

"Yeah," I say. But I'm waiting for him to pull something. "You can run away like a scared little rabbit, and we won't hurt you."

Mick looks at me and asks seriously, "Really? How about running like a big, scared gazelle?"

"A what?"

"A gazelle. It's a kind of antelope. It runs fast and is really quite graceful."

Matt looks at him as if he's crazy, and I say, "Yeah, Sullivan, run like a scared gazelle. This I gotta see."

"Okay," Mick says. "I'll try to imitate the graceful gazelle, but I'm pretty big and clumsy, so I might not pull it off. Here I go."

He runs away down the sidewalk. He glances back and does these stupid-looking leaps. But he's so big, he barely clears the ground and looks more like an elephant trying to dance ballet. He does that all the way down the street and around the corner till we can't see him behind some buildings.

We all look at each other.

"What's with that guy?" Matt asks. "He's a maniac."

"Yeah," I say. "But he got away without a fight."

They all look at me. "Hey, yeah," J.K. says.

After we throw the football around for a while, I go home. Moose meets me at the back door the way he always does, hopping around on hind legs, his tongue hanging out, yipping his head off. Moose is a poodle-and-cocker-spaniel mix, so his name is wishful thinking on my brother's part. He's almost too cute to be real, and he's never happier than when he's licking your face or running to bring back a ball you threw.

I let him out in the backyard and turn on MTV. Then I go to the kitchen for something to eat. I know there's a half-eaten bag of chips somewhere under some stuff on the table, so I start pushing things around looking for it. I find it under a plastic Wal-Mart bag that has cigarettes, beer, and dog food in it. Most of the chips underneath are crushed, but I pick up the bag and head back to the living room and sit on the couch.

Nobody's home, as usual. Mom took off three years ago, and Dad says "Good riddance" every time her name comes up. He says she was throwing our money away at the reservation casino in Boonville, anyway, so even though she cleaned out our account at the bank before she left, it's good we're rid of her.

I miss her, even though she wasn't home much. I don't tell my dad that, though. He blows up every time he thinks about her, and when he's mad, it's good to stay out of his way.

I watch MTV for the next hour till my brother gets home from work. Ethan busts in through the back door and throws a greasy bag from McDonald's onto the couch. He never brings me dinner, so I know it's not for me, but it smells like fries, and I start to open it.

"Don't even *think* about stealing a fry," he says and goes to the kitchen. He comes back holding a can of soda, and now he's shirtless and holding a magazine. He tosses it at me. "I'm finished with it," he says. "Thought you'd want it."

It's a magazine about rock stars. "Thanks," I say.

He sits at the other end of the couch, opens the soda, and eats his cheeseburger and fries. I look through the magazine and wish I had a cheeseburger, too.

Ethan graduated from high school last spring and since then has worked as a mechanic at Dalby Motors. It's a pretty good job, but he mostly talks about how much he hates his boss.

I sit there and look over at Ethan a couple of times. Last summer he got a serious tattoo that spreads over his shoulders. It's a dragon that breathes fire—the tail alone covers all of one shoulder. It's pretty cool, I think, and I figure I'll get a tattoo when I'm older. It'd be cool to play my guitar onstage, and everyone could see the tattoos on my arms under all those bright lights. I'll lift weights, too, and bulk up, and I'll have bodyguards who follow me everywhere, just in case someone thinks he can jump me. I guess rock stars can be targets for all the weirdos out there.

My dad comes home at six thirty, and he brings a pizza, so at least I can eat. He doesn't like MTV much, so I change the channel. He likes the news, so I switch to MSNBC.

Ethan gets up, fishing a pack of cigarettes out of his pocket. He taps one out and lights it. "I'm going for gas," he says. Dad says okay, and he leaves.

Dad and I don't talk. I sneak a sideways look at him. He's watching a story about the Middle East and eating his sausage pizza with extra cheese. His face is flat from this angle, kind of like someone smashed him there with a shovel. From the side, his face looks like a cartoon character.

That makes me think of what Sullivan said about how I remind him of Yosemite Sam from the cartoons, and I get mad all over again. I want to tell Dad about it, but it's a good idea to figure out what kind of mood he's in before I tell him anything. Even when he's in a good mood, it can change in a second if he gets irritated—even at himself. A couple weeks ago, he accidentally dropped a jar of pickles. It crashed on the floor. You should've heard the shouting and swearing. I've been wearing shoes in the kitchen ever since, in case not all of the glass pieces got cleaned up.

The phone rings in the kitchen after we've eaten half the pizza, so I go answer it.

"Hello, is this Boot?" the voice asks. It's a deep voice.

"Yeah."

"This is Mr. Maddox."

"Oh." My mind does this hiccup thing, and for a second I can't think who he is.

"Remember, I told you I'd explain to your parents about the game room."

The principal.

"Oh, yeah."

"Is your dad home?"

"Yeah."

"Who is it?" my dad asks from the living room.

I put down the phone and go to the doorway between the kitchen and living room.

"It's the new principal," I say.

"What's he want?"

"To talk to you."

"You do something?" He goes to the kitchen. "Hello?"

I only hear his half of the conversation, which goes something like this: "Yeah . . . yeah . . . He did?" He turns and looks at me. I can't tell what he's thinking, but at least he doesn't look too mad. "Okay," he says. "Yeah, I don't care. Bye."

He puts the phone down and stares at me. "You and the Sullivan kid got in a fight, and he's making you play *games*? What kind of stupid idea is that?"

I shrug.

Dad walks back to the living room and sits down. He doesn't say any more.

Ten minutes later, after the pizza is gone and he's smoking a cigarette and I'm sure he's forgotten about the call, he says, "What does he think'll happen, you two playing games? You and that kid have never gotten along. If he punches you, you fight back, you hear me? Don't let that giant think he can push you around just because he's bigger than you."

"I don't let people push me around," I tell him.

"Principal want you to kill each other?" He kind of grunts, takes a drag on his cigarette, and stares at the TV. "If someone gets killed, he'll have a lawsuit on his hands so fast, his head'll spin."

I don't say anything, but I'm glad he doesn't get mad enough to throw something.

"You just show that kid who's boss."

"I will," I say.

He takes another drag, and we don't talk after that.

After I'm done eating, I walk over to River City Music to see if Jesse's around. It's about two miles away. The air is cool, and it feels good on my face. I like this time of day. It's still light, but the sun is lower, and shadows stretch out long and dark on the street.

About a block away from the shop, I can see the lights are on inside; from less than a half block away, I start to hear music. When I get there, I open the door. Jesse's playing his Fender Stratocaster. Man, he can make it wail. He's singing one of his own songs, and it's better than a lot of stuff you hear on the radio.

The amp is turned up loud, but not too loud. The old man who lives over the vacuum cleaner place two doors down called the cops on Jesse last spring, so he keeps it quieter now when he plays.

The door's unlocked, so I go in. He sees me and nods, but he keeps playing and singing till the song is over.

"That was great," I say.

"Thanks," he answers. "I haven't given it to the guys yet. The lyrics at the bridge could use some work, but I'm about ready to play it for them and see what they think."

"Don't worry, Jesse," I say. "They'll like it."

The phone rings, and he goes and picks it up. "Hey, Gail!" he says. He looks really happy to hear from her, whoever she is. He turns his back to me and lowers his voice a little. "Yeah. Really? Well, we're playing next week. You wanna come? I could get you in without a cover. You could be a roadie." He laughs.

He talks a long time; it feels like forever. I get out one of the guitar catalogs from the desk next to the cash register. I turn the pages, but I don't pay a lot of attention to the pictures. I've seen them about fifty times before; I just want something to do while Jesse's turned around, talking to Gail.

Finally he turns back so he's facing me again. I think maybe he's about to get off the phone. He says, "Just a sec," into the phone, and he covers the receiver with his hand. "Hey, Boot?"

"Yeah?" I toss the catalog back on the desk.

"Uh, I'm going to be on the phone for a while. Then I've got to go home. I got a psych test tomorrow. You wanna come back in a day or two? I'll have more time then. You can try out our new Fenders." He points to the guitars standing in the corner of the window display. I hadn't even noticed them.

"Oh, yeah," I say, standing up. "That'd be cool. Well—" He looks kind of impatient, so I say, "See you."

He holds up a hand for a second and turns around again.

"Sorry," he says real quiet into the phone. Then he laughs.

I let myself out and walk back home.

CHAPTER FOUR

Mick's Turn

I DON'T KNOW WHERE the gazelle thing came from. But as I said before, I'm not a tough guy. I was being totally honest when I told them I was scared. After all, there were four of them blocking the sidewalk, ready to fight me.

As you might've guessed, I'm not proud, either. I'd be willing to bet a lot of money that I looked like an idiot leaping down the sidewalk like that. But at least it kept them from beating up on me. I might like to push Boot's buttons, but I'm not stupid.

Sometimes when Boot is in a fighting mood, I consider finding some healthier source of entertainment. But then I think, *nah*. Tormenting Boot is just too much fun, and sometimes a bloody nose is the price of admission.

I stop at the library, my home away from home. The first

thing you see in front is a metal statue. It's an old woman sitting on a bench with her arm wrapped around a little boy while she reads a book to him. The statue makes me think of how my mom and grandma read to me all the time when I was young. Every kid should have someone who reads to him. The old lady in the statue even looks like my grandma who died last year.

One time when I was seven, Nana and I came here, and she took a picture of me sitting on the bench on the grandmother's other side. I pretended to be straining to look at the book that she was reading to my "little brother," the kid in the statue. She had two copies made and framed: one for her, which she kept on her bedside table, and another one for me, which is on my desk at home. Nana always said that the library was our special place.

My friend Laura who works at the library loves the statue as much as I do, and believe it or not, she has a picture that her dad took of her sitting on the bench, too, when she was little.

I go inside. The library is quiet as usual, and people are working at computers, and reading in comfy chairs, and wandering through the stacks. I know most of the people who work here.

Laura usually shelves books, and sometimes I help her. You wouldn't believe how many books are in the wrong places. People take books off the shelves, look at them, and then jam them back in any old place. Sometimes I hang around where she's shelving and check the books on nearby shelves.

Laura Dellinger's a junior in high school and very pretty, but today she's wearing a rose-colored sweater that makes her look so hot, I can't believe it. I can't help staring, and when she catches me, I say, "You look very . . . uh, symmetrical today."

She laughs. "I do, hunh?"

I realize how stupid that sounded, so I hurry to explain. "I mean, you always look symmetrical. I read an article about how beauty is partly a matter of symmetry. If you get a crowd of people and draw a line down the middle of each person's face, the most beautiful people will be almost perfectly symmetrical. Babies have even responded to symmetrical faces in tests."

She'd stopped shelving to listen attentively. "You come up with the oddest bits of information." She smiled. "So my face is symmetrical? Well, that's the best news I've heard all day. Thanks."

I have this deep, dark secret, and hardly anybody knows it: I want to be a writer. Laura's the only person, other than my mom, who I've told. I'd known I could trust telling her. She's really nice, and even if she thought it was a stupid idea—you know, it's hard to make a living at it, and all that—I was pretty sure she wouldn't make fun of me. She had smiled when I told her, and she'd said, "I was thinking the other day that you'd probably become a writer when you're finished with school."

"Really?" That had surprised me. And it had made me feel great that she thought about me at *all*. I mean, I'm in eighth grade, and she's a junior. That's almost unheard of.

"You sound surprised," she had said. She'd smiled, and I'd had a sudden hope that maybe she could be interested in me—you know, like a boyfriend. "Mick, I know you pretty well. You're like the brother I never had."

"Oh." So my fantasy had given out a whimper and died on the spot. It was nice for the two seconds that it had lived so joyfully, though. After that, I decided that I could like her as a friend. And she's been a good one.

"Hey," she says now. "I saw a book the other day and I thought of you, so I put it aside."

"What is it?" I ask. Laura comes up with the best recommendations for me.

"Come here." She leads me behind the circulation desk and picks up a book on a table near the wall. "*Games People Play*," she says. "It's psychology. A writer needs to know how people behave, you know, and the kinds of things they do to get what they want. I thought it would be good for you to read."

"Hey, thanks." I take the book. "I owe you one."

"You don't owe me one," she says. "We're friends."

See what I mean? She's very nice.

I get home about the time Mom arrives. She works at Josephine's, a ladies' clothing store. Mr. Monroe calls his salespeople "associates," but Dad and I think that's just so he can get away with paying them minimum wage and no benefits. He probably thinks "associates" gives them a dignity that his crummy pay doesn't provide. Mom doesn't complain, though. She's a hard worker and always deserves better than she gets.

After she changes out of her work clothes into jeans, she starts preparing supper. I've taken off my shoes—I hate wearing shoes—and I'm lying on the couch in the living room, reading. Reading is the way I spend most of my spare time. I have an eclectic taste in books: thrillers, science fiction, biographies, just about anything, really, except maybe manuals on motors or mechanical things like that. Mom says I was reading cereal boxes when I was four. I've read some of the classics, but I'd never admit that to anyone at school. They'd think I was a wimp or worse—an intellectual. If you're fourteen, and you've read Steinbeck and Faulkner, everyone will make fun of you. That is, if they know who Steinbeck and Faulkner *are*. I've read that to be a good writer, you have to read a lot of great books over a long time, so you absorb it into your subconscious.

Even though Mom and Laura know my dirty little secret about wanting to write, Dad has no clue. He doesn't like eggheads, which is what he calls people who like to read.

So I'm lying on the couch reading Dean Koontz's newest book, all the while keeping one eye on the clock, so I can stash the book in my room before Dad gets home. If I stop at five thirty-five, I'm usually safe. He normally gets home at five forty-five, when he's not drinking. If he stops at a bar on his way home, then his arrival time is . . . well, your guess is as good as mine. It could be two hours later, or, on one of his benders, two days later.

Dad isn't drinking so far this week, and I finish a chapter at five thirty, so I mark my place, get up, walk down the hall, and toss the book on my bed.

"What's new at school?" Mom asks me when I wander into the kitchen. "Don't touch that!" She gently slaps my hand as I lift the lid on a pot on the stove. "It's brown rice, and you're supposed to leave the lid on while it cooks."

"Okay." I snatch a slice of strawberry and a grape off the top of the fruit salad she's making.

I get my height from both Mom and Dad. She stands about five feet ten inches and is slender with very long legs. I saw a picture of her when she was in high school, and I have to say that she was a total babe. She's smart, too, and went to college for a while. If she hadn't met Dad at a party one night in her sophomore year, she'd have graduated with a degree in English. Of course, if she had fulfilled her educational ambitions, I wouldn't be here. And frankly, I hate to think of a world without me in it.

"So? Tell me about school." She's chopping an apple on a wooden cutting board.

"Well, the biggest piece of news at school is that we have a new principal."

"Who is it?" *Chop, chop, chop.*

"His name's Maddox."

Mom looks up and back down. "You like him?" *Chop, chop.*

"Yeah, so far. He actually seems like a nice guy. I wonder where they found him?"

Mom laughs. "That's so unusual? A nice principal?" She dumps the apple pieces on top of the bowl with the sliced strawberries and grapes.

"Sure. He looks like a fullback, but he actually has some imagination."

"How so?"

"Well, he's decided that Boot Quinn and I should play board games until we can get along."

Mom stops everything and her eyes widen. "Please don't tell me you're fighting again."

"Oh, that's blown way out of proportion," I tell her. "We just had a disagreement—he's such a hothead—and we did some harmless shoving." I shrug. "No big deal."

"Mick, if you get suspended one more time—"

I hold up a hand. "I won't get suspended," I tell her.

"Well, I didn't get a call at work today," she says. "I guess that's a good sign."

The phone rings. The timing couldn't have been worse.

The sharp look she gives me says *this better not be the principal,* and she goes to the phone on the wall and answers, just as my dad walks through the kitchen door.

"Hello?" A second goes by, and she turns to look at me and gives me a stern nod. *It's the principal.*

"Yes? Yes."

"Who's that?" my dad asks. His hair's messed up, and he runs a hand sideways over his head to push it down. He takes his wallet out of his pocket, puts it on the kitchen table, goes to the cupboard, and takes down a glass.

"He did?" Mom says. She shakes her head at me and sighs, then turns away. "I'm sorry. I've run out of ideas."

Dad opens the freezer and puts ice from the bin into the glass. "Who is it?" he asks her again. He closes the freezer section, opens the refrigerator door, and takes out a Diet Pepsi. He leaves the fridge door open and pours the Pepsi into the glass.

"I think it's the new principal," I murmur.

"Why's he calling?" His stare is intense and somewhat hopeful. "You fighting again?"

I shrug. "Sort of."

"Hunh." He puts away the Pepsi and closes the fridge door.

Actually, it's Mom who hates it that I fight. For Dad, it's

the only evidence he can cling to that I might not be a sissy after all.

Mom nods as if Mr. Maddox can see her. "Well, that's an interesting idea."

The principal has just explained his games concept—I'd put money on it.

"Okay. Yes, I understand. Maybe that'll work. Okay, well, thanks for calling."

She puts the phone down and turns to me. "Another fight? Oh, Mick. Why do you continue to do this?"

"Is it that Quinn kid again?" Dad asks.

"Yeah. He's such a crabby guy."

Mom makes a sound of exasperation. "He's a crabby guy, and for that, you get in a fight with him? Come on, Mick. That doesn't make sense."

"He taunt you?" Dad asks.

No, Dad. He just called you "garbage."

"It's no big deal," I say.

Mom looks at Dad. "This is a new principal. He's having the boys get together to play games, so they'll learn how to get along. I don't know; maybe it'll help. Nothing else seems to work."

He makes a face. "Well, he's an idiot," he says. "Boys don't solve things by playing games."

"I totally agree," I say. I turn to Mom. "We ready for din-din?"

She frowns because I've changed the subject. "Not yet. About five minutes."

Dad lifts the lid on the pot with the rice to peek inside, but Mom doesn't slap *his* hand. "What're we having?" he asks.

"Roasted chicken," she says.

Dad mutters in response while he takes off his khakis and white shirt with HOME HARDWARE AND GARDEN stitched in red letters on the pocket. He drops his clothes on the floor just outside the kitchen and walks down the hall to his bedroom wearing only his underwear. Dad hates wearing clothes other than underwear, but Mom insists he wear at least jeans and a T-shirt.

She sees his discarded clothes, sighs, and scoops them up off the floor. She walks down the hall to the bedroom, and I hear her plead her case one more time about the dropped clothes that she has to pick up. I don't know why she wastes her breath, but she never seems to give up hope. He promises to start hanging up his clothes, but he never does. I doubt he ever will. It's part of his passive-aggressive personality, I guess. He makes the same promise about drinking.

We eat dinner on TV trays and watch a stand-up comic on Comedy Central. He isn't funny, but Dad laughs anyway, and Mom smiles at him. She's always happy when he's on the wagon because we seem like a real family.

After we've eaten, Dad turns to me and says, "Why don't

you and me go out and play some catch?"

"Uh . . . I have homework to do," I say. "But thanks."

"Come on," he says. "You can do your homework when we're through playing. You could use some physical activity. You spend too much time loafing around."

He doesn't say *"and reading,"* but I'm guessing that's what he's thinking.

I avoid Mom's look. I know her face is saying *"Do it for your dad."*

"Okay," I say. Sometimes it's easier to give in than to argue. I'd probably end up going outside with him in the end, anyway. I figure I might as well get it over with.

He goes to get the mitts and a ball from his closet, and I put on my sneakers and wait for him in the kitchen.

"He wants to spend time with you," Mom says in a low voice. She runs water in the sink.

"He wants to make a man out of me," I say. "A macho man, and it's not my style. Don't you need help with the dishes or something?"

She rolls her eyes. "I can handle the dishes."

Dad strides through the kitchen. "Let's go," he says. He tosses me the second mitt.

"Okay." I give Mom a resigned salute and follow him out the back door.

Our backyard slopes uphill at the back, so it's not the best place to play catch. "We'll do this sideways," Dad says, gesturing for me to move to the grassy area behind the garage.

The sun, a fiery globe, is hanging in the sky just above Dad's head, so I squint. "I can't see you very well," I say.

"Ballplayers have to get used to all kinds of situations," he says, ignoring the rather important detail that I'm not a ballplayer. He throws me the ball, but because I don't see it coming, it flies over my head and hits the garage.

"I can't see it," I say. "The sun's in my eyes."

"Hold up your mitt to block the sun," he says.

I pick up the ball and throw it back to him.

"You have a good arm," he says. "You should be playing ball."

He's told me this before, so I say what I always say. "Thanks, but I don't enjoy it. And I can't run fast, and I'm pretty uncoordinated."

"You could work on those things," he says. He throws the ball back to me.

This time, I see it coming and hold out my arm. The ball, like a missile, zeros in on the target, and plops right into the mitt. And bounces out and hits the ground.

"I don't think you can learn coordination," I tell him. I pick up the ball and throw it back. "I think it's something you're born with, like perfect pitch."

"You're just not trying," he says.

He sounds pretty frustrated, and I feel sorry for maybe the four thousandth time that I can't be an athlete for him. His high-school baseball team won the state championship when he was a senior, and I know he always hoped he could relive his glory days through me.

"Maybe you and Mom should have another kid," I tell him. "Maybe you'll luck out next time and get a little Hall of Famer."

Dad doesn't bother to answer, but I can see by the look on his face that he aches down to the bone for the athletic son he never had.

CHAPTER FIVE

Boot's Turn

I GET TO THE principal's office at eleven the next morning, and Mick's already there. I've been kind of nervous, thinking about having to play games with him, and by now I'm pretty mad that this stupid principal is caging us together. I *hate* Mick Sullivan, and no amount of playing games will change my mind—unless he somehow gets a personality transplant in the next few days.

I'll have to remember that: a personality transplant. It's pretty funny, and I figure I can say it to him when he thinks he's being real smart.

Mick is sitting in one of the plastic chairs in the outer office. As soon as I see him, I turn my head so I don't have to look at him, and I sit down in the chair that's farthest away. Mrs. Taylor, who's at her desk behind the counter, looks up and scowls at me, which is her usual way of telling you she knows you're here.

She gets up and goes to the doorway to the principal's office and says something that I can't hear. Then she sits down, and the principal comes out.

"Good morning," he says. He comes around the counter.

Sullivan kind of mutters, "Morning," and I just nod.

"Come on back," he says. "The game room's ready to go."

Mick and I get up and follow him in. The room has two doors. One leads in from the principal's office, and the other goes to the mail room. I stop and look around. I've gotten glimpses of this room before. It used to have stuff like file cabinets, shelves with piles of books and papers, and boxes full of junk.

But now it looks like somebody's crummy living room. In the middle of the room is a ratty couch. A beat-up coffee table stands in front of it, and board games are piled on it. I can see Battleship, Jenga, Connect Four, Scrabble, and checkers in a stack, and three decks of cards on the very top of the pile.

A stuffed chair like my grandma has, only this one's in really bad shape, sits on this side of the coffee table. An old desk with a crappy-looking lamp on it is pushed against the wall, and a big, worn-out rug is stretched out on the floor.

A bunch of plants are sitting around the room, too. And that's pretty much it. Oh, yeah—and there aren't any windows.

The principal pushes the big chair closer to the coffee table.

"Okay, have a seat."

I take the big chair, so Mick goes to the couch and sits down.

"I can't help you with this," he says. "You'll work it out between the two of you. The only rule I have is that you take care of the furniture and play games."

I wonder why we have to take care of the furniture. I don't think the Salvation Army would even want this stuff.

I look quick at Mick. He's staring at the pile of games.

"Which game do you want to start with?" the principal asks.

I don't say anything, so Mick goes, "How about Authors?"

"Okay with you, Boot?"

I don't know any game called Authors, so I shrug.

He picks up the decks of cards. "We have Classic Authors and American Authors." He looks at me. "Which will it be?"

I don't know what Classic Authors is, so I shrug again. "American, I guess."

"Okay with you, Mick?"

"Yeah," he says.

He hands Mick one of the packs of cards. "I'll be next door in my office."

He walks out of the room. Mick moves the pile of games to the floor. He kicks off his shoes and picks up one of the decks of cards. He rips off the cellophane wrapper. I get a whiff of something horrible. Then I realize what it is.

"Your feet stink," I say. "I can smell them clear over here."

His eyebrows go up. "They're my secret weapon. They can kill at twenty paces."

"Put your shoes on, Sullivan," I say. "Or I'm not playing."

He doesn't put on his shoes, and he smiles. I watch him shuffle the cards, and I realize we're about to play a game, and I don't know how to play it. I should've said I don't want to play this game. I know he'll just try to teach it to me and act like a big shot if I don't get it right away. So I stand up and go over to the desk next to the wall and sit on it.

"What're you doing?" Mick asks.

"I'm sitting on this desk, you moron," I say. I give myself a point on the scorecard in my head for zinging him. "Your feet stink, and I'm not playing."

He rolls his eyes. "Come on, Boot. This is easier than a suspension." He pauses, and I know he's watching me. "Okay, Boot. You win. I'll put my shoes back on."

I don't answer, and from the corner of my eye I see him putting on his shoes.

"There," he says. "I can't imagine why you hate the smell of my feet. People tell me they wish they could patent the fragrance to make exotic and expensive perfume. But you can't smell them now. The shoes are on."

I still don't move, and I don't say anything.

"Okay. Fine. We won't play." He reaches back and tries to get something out of his pocket. It won't budge. He stands up and pulls harder. I stare at him. He tugs with one hand, then tries it with both hands. Then he yanks it out. A paperback. He looks at me like he's mad. "So? My jeans shrank in the wash."

I snort and shake my head like I think he's really pathetic. "You're such a nerd," I say.

"Thank you," he says. He flops on the couch, opens his book, and starts reading.

I sit there for a while, but pretty soon I'm bored. I swing my legs a little and kick the desk. He doesn't seem to notice.

A while later, the principal pokes his head in the door. "Why aren't you playing Authors?"

"He won't play," says the narc.

"Come over here, Boot," he tells me. "You're here to work on getting along." He picks up the opened deck of cards. He suddenly stops and turns to stare at me. "I just realized that we didn't go over the rules."

I relax a little because I know now that if he gets us started and tells us the rules, I'll probably be okay. So I get off the desk and go sit in the big chair.

You should see him shuffle the deck—like he plays poker every night, or he's an expert in Las Vegas or something. Even Mick's eyes are big, watching him.

He deals four cards to each of us and sets the deck face-down on the table. "This is like Go Fish. The deck has thirteen authors with four cards each. Okay, so pick up your four cards. Instead of looking at the numbers and suits, you look at the authors and their books."

I pick mine up, and I have two cards with a picture of this guy wearing a nerdy bow tie named Theodore something, one card with a lady whose last name is Welty, and another card with a guy in a mustache named William F— I don't know how to pronounce it, either. Man, aren't there any American authors named Smith? Or White? Or Johnson?

"Okay," he says, "each of these authors has four books listed. You have the book that's listed at the top of the card. You want to collect the cards of all four of their books. Those are the titles listed at the bottom. The player with the largest number of an author's complete set of books at the end of the game wins. Okay?"

Now I see why the game is like Go Fish, so I say, "Yeah. I know how to play."

"Good." Then he says, "I was just reminded about a meeting I have down at the schoolboard building. So let Mrs. Taylor know if you need anything. At eleven forty-three, you'll go down and get your lunches and bring them back here to eat. At twelve ten, when the bell rings, you'll go back to your classes. Okay?"

"Okay," Mick says.

He nods. "Great. See you later."

"Yeah," Mick says along with a sigh. He sounds bored already, and I hate him.

The principal leaves, and Mick says, "I'll go first."

I don't know why he thinks he can decide who goes first, but I decide not to say anything. I stare at my cards and realize that I'm going to have to say the authors' names out loud. And I don't know how to pronounce them.

"Do you have Eugene O'Neill's *The Iceman Cometh?*"

I look over my cards again, but I don't have any of that guy's books. "No."

He picks the top card off the pile. "Didn't get it. Your turn."

"Do you have—" I look closer at my cards and decide just to say the name the way it looks. Maybe Mick won't know how to pronounce it either. "Theodore Dre— Dreiser's book *Sister Carrie.*"

I wait and he doesn't say anything. I look up. He's watching me, and his eyebrows go up.

"So you have it or not?" I say.

"No," he says.

I pick a card off the top of the deck. It's another of that William guy. I take back what I said about the principal's shuffling. What he did looked good, but the cards aren't shuffled the way they should be. Maybe he didn't shuffle them enough.

"Do you have *Moby Dick* by Herman Melville?" he asks.

"No."

He draws a card.

I sit there, look at my cards, and decide to go with the lady author, even though I'll probably say her name wrong. "*The Robber Bridegroom* by Eudora Welty."

Again, he doesn't say anything. So I look up. "Yes or no?" It comes out sounding madder than I mean.

He rolls his eyes and says, "No."

I draw. "Got it," I say, but it comes out kind of excited, and I don't mean to sound like that, either.

Then I see that I got the right author, but the wrong book. We just started, and already I messed up. My face gets hot, and I stare at the cards in my hands, wondering what I should do. They get fuzzy as my eyes unfocus.

"What?" he says.

"What?" I say.

"You're turning red," he says and laughs. "I can't believe it. You're *blushing*."

"Shut up," I say. I knew he'd take the first chance possible to make fun of me. I want to knock his head off. I almost reach over to punch him, but I stop myself. "Why don't you just go get a personality transplant?" I say.

"Because I'd rather donate the money to get *you* one. I bet everyone you know would thank me, starting with your family."

"Just wait till after school."

"Well, I'm not scared, Boot, and you know why? Because all I'd have to do is knock you down and sit on your puny chest, and if I didn't push all the air out of your lungs and suffocate you, I'd at least render you completely helpless."

"*Render* me?" I say. "How long did it take you to work *that* word into a conversation, brainiac?" Another zinger, and I realize that even with a red face, I'm racking up points on that scorecard in my head.

"So why are you blushing?" he asks.

"Forget it."

"You're a weird guy, Yosemite," he says. I open my mouth, but he holds up his hand. "Okay, okay. Let's just play. If you got what you asked for—*The Robber Bridegroom*, was it?—you get to ask again."

I look at my cards. "Do you have that same lady's book, *Delta Wedding*?"

"No."

I pick up the card on the top of the deck, hoping it'll be a name I can pronounce. *Finally*. Robert Frost. I even heard of him.

He goes, "Do you have Thomas Wolfe's *Look Homeward, Angel*?"

"No."

He picks up the top card and stares at it. "I thought you said you got *Robber Bridegroom* when you drew a card last time."

I don't know what to say. "I did," slips out in a little voice.

"Well, that's pretty interesting, because *I* just got it." He flips the card around and shows it to me. I expect him to call me a moron, but instead he gets this little smile and says: "So *that's* why you were blushing."

I feel my face getting hot all over again, and I'm starting to sweat.

"Man, you should see your face," he says, laughing. You're redder than before. Tough guy Boot Quinn is *blushing*."

I throw my cards on the floor and scream at him that I'm not playing anymore. I get up, not even thinking what I'm doing, and I go over to the wall and punch it hard. Pain rips through my hand, and I wonder if I broke a finger, but I bite down hard and stuff my hand under my other armpit and turn my face and lean into the wall, so he can't see. Tears come from the pain, and I close my eyes to keep the water inside, but it spills out onto my face.

I think he says something, but I don't hear what.

I push off the wall, cross the room, and walk out the door, through the office, and around the corner. Mrs. Taylor isn't at her desk, so she doesn't see me leave. I shove the outside door open with my good hand and keep walking until I'm halfway down the block. The alley is the shortest route home, so I take it.

* * *

When I get home, I let Moose outside and go down the basement stairs and into my room. I put on my headphones and turn my CD player up as loud as I can take it. It thunders into my head and vibrates through my body. I close my eyes and concentrate till I block out everything but the music.

CHAPTER SIX

Mick's Turn

THAT WAS A BIG SURPRISE, Boot walking out. But a bigger surprise was when he blushed. And the biggest surprise of all was when he slammed his bare knuckles into the wall. He's always been a crabby guy and a hothead, but I've never seen him hurt *himself.* Normally he hurts somebody else.

I wonder if he crushed any bones in his hand. He had enough force behind the punch that it's definitely possible.

That's gotta hurt.

Even *I* would've screamed in agony, and I have what must be a record-high tolerance for pain. (If I didn't, I wouldn't be willing to harass Boot till he starts whomping on me.) But I would've had a hard time taking the pain he must've felt when his fist hit that wall.

Amazingly, Boot didn't make a sound, except for that one

low noise, like a wounded animal, just afterward. I wouldn't have believed it if I hadn't seen it myself.

But man, is he sensitive. . . . When he pronounced Theodore Dreiser's name "Theodore *Dress*er," and I corrected him, he pretended he didn't hear me. I wasn't trying to act like a smart guy. I even said it in a whisper, so he wouldn't think I was making fun. And then again, when he pronounced Eudora Welty's first name as "*Ee-oo*-dora," and I murmured, "Yoo-dora," he ignored me again.

I was just trying to help him.

But I see now why it's so easy to rile him. He didn't want to admit that he'd blushed. I guess he thinks it's not macho and would ruin his reputation as a tough guy if I knew he'd cried. I said, "Okay, Boot, let's start over again," but he wasn't interested. I didn't know that he was crying till he stalked out, and I saw that his face was wet.

I get up from the couch and go to the game-room door, wondering if Mrs. Taylor saw Boot leave. She's not at her desk. She probably went outside to smoke. I've seen her standing out on the loading dock with Ms. Derby, the head custodian, their cigarettes chugging two trails of smoke into the air.

Once, while standing on the other side of a nearby tree, I overheard them talking about Boot and me and the fights we'd had. Mrs. Taylor said we should be expelled, and Ms. Derby agreed and said she'd thought of offering her services to Mr. Block to box our ears. They laughed and then stopped to hack away with their cigarette coughs.

So anyway, I see that Mr. Maddox hasn't come back from his meeting, and Mrs. Taylor's gone, too. I wonder what I should do. If I go back to class, Ms. Pruitt, my language arts teacher, will know I'm not in the game room. If I go home, Mr. Maddox will find out, and I'll get in trouble for leaving. I decide to take the path of least resistance. I walk back to my paperback, flop on the couch, and open my book to read. I look at my watch and see that I have nearly an hour before my game-room time is up. Time to read. It's the best news I've had all day.

Mrs. Taylor pokes her head in a half hour later and says, "Where's Boot?"

I look up from my reading and shrug. "Beats me. I guess you'll have to ask him."

"You mean he walked out?"

"Uh-hunh."

"When?"

I look at the clock. "About thirty minutes ago."

She rolls her eyes. "Well, you just stay there," she says. She looks angry.

"Hey, no problem," I say.

A minute later, I hear her on the phone in her office. I get up and walk quietly to the doorway and listen.

She's saying, "So what did I tell you? He's crazy, putting these two wild kids together. I knew it wouldn't work." She laughs. "Care for a little wager?" She listens a moment, then says, "I'll do better than that. I say within a week, the boys are suspended, and Maddox figures out he's got to get tough with these kids. A dinner at Red Lobster? Great, it's a bet." She laughs again. "See you later." She hangs up, and I scramble back to the couch.

She comes to the doorway. "You better go back to your class," she says. "I'll give you a hall pass."

It doesn't take long for the word to spread around school that Boot and I have to play games. Someone asks me about it probably ten times that day. I smile and say, "Boot Quinn will do *anything* to spend more time with me." It always gets a laugh; everyone knows that Boot hates my guts.

It isn't until Tabitha Slater walks up to me in the hall later that afternoon that I realize how famous I'm getting because of the game room. I mean, *Tabitha Slater*? Talking to *me*? She usually reserves her attention for the jocks and cool guys.

I'm surprised she even knows I'm alive.

It's after fifth-period science class, and I'm standing behind a guy at the water fountain. I think this kid must be slurping up the town's entire water supply. I'm thinking about giving up and coming back later, when this small blonde thing sashays into my peripheral vision. I'm thunder-struck.

I've looked at her straight-on enough times to know for sure that it's Tabitha. As a general rule, she gets around by walking at a casual stroll with her hips swaying from side to side. Watching her could make a guy dizzy.

"Hey, Mike, I heard about you!" she says.

I turn to face her and manage to say, "Mick." It comes out like a squeak, and I clear my throat.

She laughs and beams her megawatt-and-braces smile at me. I'm nearly blinded. Either that or maybe lightning struck; who knows?

"Mike, Mick. Whatever." She shrugs her little shoulders. (Man, even her shoulders are cute.) "I hear you and Boot Quinn have to play games every day."

I open my mouth, but nothing comes out. I've never in my life been struck speechless before this; but then, I've never had a conversation with Tabitha Slater before. I'm astonished at the control she has over my brain. She has single-handedly shut down the part that controls speech.

I give her a mushy-mouthed, "Umm-hunh."

She laughs. "It's so funny. Aren't you the guys who fight all the time?"

"Yeah," I manage to say. Then I add, willing my mouth to form speech, "It's our hobby."

She laughs again, louder. The guy who consumed

enough water at the fountain to fill a lake is now finished. He straightens up and wipes his mouth on his T-shirt. But I don't care now, because I'm committed to keeping this conversation going as long as I can—even if I die of thirst right here in front of her.

Tabitha says, "I think I'll beat up on my best friend, too, so we'll get to play games every day. That'd be pretty cool."

"Want me to help?" I ask. "I could give you some pointers."

"Really? Pointers on how to beat her up?" She's still beaming. It's like the whole world around us drops out of sight, and all I can see is Tabitha. She seems to be standing on a dark stage in a spotlight. "So what should I keep in mind while I'm punching her lights out?"

"Oh, you know," I say. "Hit below the belt, pull her hair, bite her if you can. The usual stuff."

She laughs again. Man, what a great laugh. "If I did that, I'd get a bad rep like yours," she says. "But if I could get to play games every day, it might be worth it."

Little does she know that Boot and I came very close to fighting over *her* about two months ago. It was in July when the three of us went swimming at the Balley Park Pool. We didn't go together, of course. We just happened to be in the same pool at the same time, although, in my opinion, that fact gives me bragging rights to claim that I went swimming with her.

Anyway, I got to the pool that day and saw that she was sitting on the sundeck, along with two of her friends, Abby and Cheyanne. So instead of leaving my towel in a heap to go dive into the water the way I usually do, I went to a bench nearby and sat on it. I positioned myself so I only had to turn my head just a tiny bit to see Tabitha. I congratulated myself; I could watch her without being too obvious.

The girls were taking turns slathering sunscreen all over each other's backs. They were already pretty tan, especially on their shoulders and noses, and I allowed my mind to play with a little fantasy.

I'm sitting next to Tabitha, and she turns to me and says, "Mick, would you put this on my back?" She hands the tube of white stuff to me and pulls her blonde hair forward over her shoulder, so I have an unobstructed area of skin to grease. She looks back over her shoulder and smiles. "Don't miss any spots."

You can bet I wouldn't.

But just as I was getting to the best part of the fantasy— namely, rubbing my hand over her back, which fortunately for me at the moment didn't have a shirt on it—I heard a familiar voice call out, "Hey, fatso, get out of my sun. You're blocking the rays."

I looked over and saw big-mouth Boot Quinn, who was sitting with Matt, Clay, and Jerrod. He scowled at me and his buddies laughed.

I didn't point out that I'm not fat—I'm pleasingly husky,

thank you very much—because it seemed an unimportant detail at the moment. The important thing was the fact that I was sitting in the vicinity of the cutest girl in school and two of her popular friends, and four guys were obviously warming up to give me a bad time right in front of her.

I looked up at the sky and tried to stay calm. "I'm not in your sun, Boot. At this particular moment, it's nearly straight overhead."

Then I realized that while I wasn't blocking Boot's sun, I *was* blocking his view of Tabitha. I'd seen him staring at her in the hall at school before. He usually looked feverish and nearly panting, he was so thrilled to see her.

(I know the feeling, so I'm not making fun of him . . . exactly.)

Boot and his buddies put their heads together, then got up and, scuffing their feet along the cement, walked over to my bench.

"Get off the sundeck," Boot said.

"It's a free country, Boot." I looked away, wondering if I'd created too much bad karma by tormenting Boot in the past. The payback would be especially hard to take if it involved humiliation in front of these girls.

"We say you go," Boot said. The four of them went behind my bench and shoved it so it toppled over. I landed on the cement with the bench on top of me. Boot and his buddies laughed.

In my peripheral vision I saw Tabitha and her friends pause in their slathering to watch. Now I *couldn't* back down or I'd look like a wimp. Worse than a wimp: a *giant* wimp. I decided that "divide and conquer" might be the best strategy, so I went after Boot. I picked him up—he couldn't have weighed more than a hundred pounds—walked off the deck with him screaming in my ear, went straight to the pool, and threw him in the deep end. The lifeguard blew his whistle at me, but I ignored him. Even though I was probably two or three years younger, I was bigger than he was, so I figured he wouldn't confront me. And he didn't, which was a wise move on his part, because the stakes were particularly high while I was under observation by the aforementioned Tabitha Slater.

The girls on the sundeck were laughing, so I smiled and waved to them. I realized then that with four guys against me I'd probably either get beaten up, or I'd have to retreat and look really bad. Now was the best time to leave.

But when I was out in the parking lot, I called on my cell phone to the swimming pool office and asked that Mick Sullivan be paged on the loudspeaker to come to the telephone. That way, Boot and his friends—or Tabitha and her friends, on the off-chance that any of them knew my name—would think I'd been paged. See? This way I wasn't *running away*. I was being a dutiful son, which I sort of am, whenever it's convenient.

A guy's gotta do what a guy's gotta do to save face.

Anyway, now Tabitha's standing there in front of me in the hallway, and she's still smiling.

"I guess I'll let you and Boot do the fighting," she says. "The rest of us will have fun watching."

"Hey," I say, cocking my eyebrow and hoping I look reasonably cool. "I'm always interested in providing top-level entertainment."

She whoops with laughter again, and a little aircraft somewhere in my chest takes flight. Really. It feels like that, anyway.

"But Boot walked out on me today," I say.

"He walked out?" Tabitha's eyes get bigger, if that's possible. "You mean he walked right out of the room where you were supposed to be playing games?"

"Yeah," I say. "You know Boot. Always the hothead."

"Wow," she says. "He'll get *so* suspended for that. Did he leave school?"

"With Boot, you never know what to expect," I say.

"Come on, Tab," someone calls. "We gotta get to science before the bell rings."

It's Cheyanne, who's heading down the hall at full tilt.

"Well, have fun in the game room tomorrow," Tabitha says. "See ya."

"Yeah, see ya," I say.

Wow. This game-room experience is really paying off in ways I never imagined.

I take a deep breath, let it out, and head down the hall toward language arts class. I feel like *skipping* down the hall, I'm so happy. Of course, I don't, and I make sure my lumber is as close to normal as possible.

It's halfway through the period before I realize my mouth tastes like the Sahara, and I remember that I never did get that drink of water.

CHAPTER SEVEN

Boot's Turn

I STAY IN MY ROOM all afternoon. My hand hurts a lot, so I'm careful with it. I don't think it's broken, but part of it's bruised pretty bad, and it's swollen in places. At one point, I go upstairs to get some ice for it, but the trays in the freezer are empty, so I fill them and stick them back in the freezer. After listening to CDs for a couple hours, I fall asleep. When I wake up, I hear someone walking around upstairs, so I go up.

Dad's home. He's already changed from his work clothes into jeans and a T-shirt that has a picture of a Harley on the front. He's never had a motorcycle, but sometimes he talks about wanting one, and he likes to ride his friend Greg's bike when he gets a chance. He punches the power button on the TV remote and sits on the couch. He hasn't brought any food with him, so I figure I'm on my own for food.

"You want some mac and cheese?" I ask. "I'll make some."

"Yeah," he says. I walk into the kitchen. "Hey," he calls out, "put lots of butter in it."

I say "Okay."

"And salt and pepper."

I say "Okay," again, and I use my good hand to get the pot off the counter and put hot water in it to boil the macaroni. I push away the pizza box from last night that's sitting on the burner, turn on the flame, and set the pot on top. Moose is jumping up and down, asking for a treat, so I give him a chewy bar, and he trots over and collapses in the corner of the kitchen. I find the box of mac and cheese on the kitchen table, rip the top off with my good hand, and hang out in the doorway to watch the news on TV.

"We get any mail?" Dad asks.

"I'll see." I go to the front door and open it. All the mail is sticking out of the mailbox. I take it inside and give it to him. Then I go back to the stove and stare into the water, waiting for it to boil.

A minute later, my dad yells "What's this?" and clomps into the kitchen, waving a piece of paper in his hand. I start to sweat.

"Who put this charge on the card?" His face is red, and he's shaking a bill in his fist. "You do this? You charge something at the Corner?"

"No," I say. "I never use your credit card." I feel a little better, knowing it's not my fault. "What's the bill for?"

"It's Ethan, then," he says. He slams the bill down on the dining room table, and I move to get out of his way. But I step back too late and bump into him. He's still so mad, he gives me a shove, and I fall back against the stove. The pot and the water—which is close to boiling—go flying. The pot lands on the floor, and the water splashes mostly over the stove and the floor, but some of it hits my arm and my jeans.

I yell loud—I can't help it, the water burns—and I quick take off my jeans and run cold water into the sink. I put my arm under the water to stop my skin from burning. With my other hand, I yank off about a yard of paper towels from the roll on the counter, get it wet, and put it on my leg with the water dripping down to the floor.

Dad grabs the phone and makes a call. He asks for Ethan, and I figure he's calling him at work. While he waits, he growls something I can't hear.

"Ethan!" he yells. "You order something at the Corner and put it on my credit card? Last month, on the eighteenth."

I look up and see my dad frown and start to say something, but he stops himself. "Oh," he says. "Okay. Well, I don't want you using my card." His voice isn't so loud now. He hangs up and shuffles back into the living room.

I think maybe the ice is ready, so I check the freezer.

With my good hand, I pry two cubes out of the plastic tray and wrap some paper towel around them. I sit in the living room and watch the news with the ice on my arm and leg. I have a bruise coming out on my arm where it must have hit the edge of the stove. It's a while later—when most of the ice has melted—that I start making the mac and cheese again.

Dad and I eat in front of the TV—we watch some old western reruns on cable—and after about a half hour, he goes, "You get burned bad?"

I tell him no. But I'm curious about what Ethan said about the credit-card bill. "What did Ethan say?"

He moves a little, like he's uncomfortable on the couch. "It was the ice I got for the poker game with Stan." He clears his throat. "I forgot about it."

He sees my swollen hand. "What's wrong with your hand?" he asks.

I shrug. "It's okay."

He looks like he just remembers something. "You start playing games with the Sullivan kid?"

"I don't want to play games with him," I say.

"That why your hand's black-and-blue? You fight him?"

I know he wants me to say yes. "Yeah."

His voice takes on an edge. "You give as good as you got?"

I don't look at him. "Yeah."

"Good. You show him."

"I did. I showed him."

* * *

The next morning, I'm dreaming about Mom when cold water pours on my head. I shoot up in bed and blink my eyes. My brain won't work right because in my head I'm still with Mom. But as I look around the room, she fades away.

Dad stands over me holding a pot from the kitchen.

"How many times do I have to tell you to get up?"

"I didn't hear you," I say and put a hand on my head. My hair is sopping wet.

"We go through this every morning," he says. "I got you a clock radio, but you sleep right through it. Turn it up *louder*, will you?" He's leaning over, shouting in my face.

"Yeah," I say.

But I know I won't. Ethan's room is upstairs, right over mine, and he doesn't have to be at work till eight thirty. He sleeps till the last minute, and if my radio wakes him up even a few minutes early, he gets really mad. A potful of water on my head from Dad isn't as bad as a smack in the face from Ethan.

Anyway, I don't have time to eat breakfast, so I leave for school. I know there's going to be questions about why I left yesterday. I figure I'll tell the principal what happened, that Sullivan made me mad, and I won't play games with him. It's like that saying, you can lead a horse to water, but you can't make it drink. I'll go to the game room, but that doesn't mean I'll play.

Let him yell, or suspend me, or kick me out of school. That wouldn't be too bad. It's still better than playing games with Mick Sullivan.

About a block away from school, I hear, "Hey, Boot," and I turn and see Tabitha Slater walking with two of her friends. She's smiling right at me, and my insides get jumpy. But I hold up my hand and say, "Hey." It's my hurt hand, but it's not too swollen now, so I doubt she'll notice.

She walks over, followed by her friends Abby and Cheyanne. She's chewing gum, and I wonder if it could get stuck all over her braces. Then I think I can't believe I'm thinking about gum when Tabitha Slater is standing right here in front of me.

She goes, "So what're you going to do in the game room today?" She laughs. "I hear you walked out yesterday."

I'm suddenly on alert. "Who told you that?"

She looks back at her friends who laugh, and then she turns back and smiles into my face again. "Well, who was in the game room with you?"

I look at these girls, and I can't tell for sure if they're making fun of me. I wonder what Mick said. *Like, did he say I cried?* I can feel my face getting hot. If Mick Sullivan was here right now, I'd make him wish he was never born.

And then Tabitha shrieks and says, "Here comes Mike now."

One of her friends says, "Mick," in a soft voice, and she says, "Oh, yeah. Mick."

So Tabitha doesn't even know his name. I figure that's a good sign, and I know this is my chance to show Tabitha that I stand up to Mick like a man.

He's walking on the sidewalk across the street with Adam and Connor, two guys in our grade. I know it's risky because I'm outnumbered, but I have to take the chance because of Tabitha. So I yell, "Hey, snotnose!"

Tabitha and her friends crack up at the name, and I feel like I suddenly grow three inches. Mick and the other guys look over and see us. I think Mick's surprised that I'm with Tabitha, 'cause he freezes for just a second. Then he gets that smile I really hate and walks across the street, stuffing his hands in his back pockets, acting like he's real cool. The other guys follow him, smiling like they think this is going to be fun.

"Boot, Boot, Boot," Mick says, shaking his head. "When they made you, they broke the mold. Then an angry mob found the mold-maker, dragged him into the street, and shot him."

Tabitha and her friends laugh, and so do Mick's friends. I know Mick is trying to look good for Tabitha, and I suddenly think: *What if he says he saw me cry yesterday?*

"Everybody's talking about you guys," Tabitha says. "You sure fight a lot."

She sounds impressed.

"As I told you yesterday," Mick says. "I only provide top-notch entertainment." He smiles at Tabitha, and she gives him this huge smile back.

"Hey, Boot," Mick says, looking at me now. "How come your hair's always wet when you come to school?"

I scowl at him. "What do you think? I *wash* it, lardbutt."

Tabitha and her friends go, *"Ooo!"* really loud.

And Mick goes, "So what do you wash it with—bacon grease?"

I'm not gonna take that, so I run at him and give him a hard shove. He moves back a few steps but doesn't fall, and he shoves me back. I knock into Tabitha, who falls on her butt with a yell.

I know right away that Mick just handed me a golden opportunity.

I go, "You leave her alone!" and I rush at Mick and tackle him. I start punching, but Adam and Connor pull me off him right away. I see that Tabitha looks at me like I'm a hero or something.

I try to pull away from those guys and yell, "You don't got a right to hurt a girl, Sullivan. This is between you and me."

I quick look at Tabitha, who's watching me with huge eyes, so I know I made a big impression.

"Hey, Boot, calm down," Mick says. "It's not like I was trying to hurt Tabitha. I'd never hurt her on purpose."

Now Tabitha looks at Mick the same way, and one of her friends laughs a little and gives her a soft punch on the arm.

"So let's just knock it off, okay?" Mick says. "Before anybody really gets hurt."

"Like you?" I say to him.

"Like anybody," he says.

I jerk my arms away from those guys who're still holding on. "Just leave her alone, Sullivan," I say. It seems like a good time to leave, so I walk off.

Besides, that final line is a good one, and I want it to be the last thing I say in front of Tabitha.

But he calls out to me when I'm across the street. "Hey, Boot! Whatever kind of look you were going for with the hair? Doesn't work, buddy. The wet look is out."

CHAPTER EIGHT

Mick's Turn

I'M BEGINNING TO think this game-room sentence is the best thing that's ever happened to me. I've never been so popular. Of course, on a scale of zero to ten, I guess it's not all that impressive to go from zero to three and a half. But if all you've ever experienced is zero, then let me tell you, the difference of a few points feels like a meteoric climb.

I don't want to give the impression that I've been an outcast. I do have friends. But they're friends-at-school friends. Situational friends. I don't see them very often outside of school because I'm usually reading at home or at the library.

But suddenly I'm Adam's and Connor's good buddy, and Tabitha Slater is looking at me as if she actually might be interested in me. I feel like a celebrity. If you'd asked me a week ago if that was remotely possible, I would've said it was more likely that I'd sprout wings and fly to the moon.

Of course, I thought Tabitha had a similar expression on her face when Boot defended her honor after I pushed him, and he staggered back and bumped her. Who knows what's going on in that pretty head of hers? I won't count on anything really great happening between her and me, but I *will* allow myself to fantasize.

A lot.

I wonder all morning what Mr. Maddox will do about Boot's leaving school yesterday. Maybe he called him at home last night and told his dad. I've never seen Judd Quinn, but I've heard that he can be a raging maniac, and I wonder how Judd might have taken the news.

At eleven o'clock, when classes are changing, I head down the hall toward the main office.

"Hey, Mick. Going to the game room?" Adam appears out of the crowd and holds up a hand, grinning.

I slap it and say, "Yeah. It's a dirty job, but somebody has to do it." He laughs, and I see some other kids smiling, too.

I get to the office and nod at Mrs. Taylor before sitting down. Boot walks in a minute later. His hair is dry now, and he hasn't combed it, as usual.

"Hey," I say to him, but he doesn't speak. He stares straight ahead. I decide not to say anything about yesterday. I'm sure Mr. Maddox will say it for me.

Mrs. Taylor sticks her head in the principal's office for a

second. Less than a minute later, Mr. Maddox lumbers out of his office.

"Come on back," he says. We get up and he leads us into the game room. "Sit down."

Here it comes.

He sits on the couch. I take a seat at the other end, and Boot flops on the big chair.

"Mrs. Taylor tells me that you left the game room yesterday, Boot," he says. "In fact, you left school."

Boot is now slumped in the chair, and he looks away. "Yeah."

"You both started to play Authors. What happened?"

Boot looks up at him, but I say, "He got mad because I teased him about blushing."

"That right?" he asks Boot.

He shrugs. "Yeah."

He turns to me, and I hold up my hands and say, "Okay, I know I shouldn't have given him a hard time. It was just kind of funny. I've never seen Boot blush before."

Boot stares over my shoulder.

"Mick," Mr. Maddox tells me, "this time in the game room is to give you experience getting along. You know how Boot probably felt when you teased him."

"Yeah," I say. "Probably not good."

"You have anything you want to say to Boot about that?"

Of course, he's asking for an apology, and I figure it's sort of justified. "Okay. I'm sorry, Boot."

"Look at *him* and say it," Mr. Maddox says.

"Yeah, okay." I turn to Boot. "I'm sorry I teased you yesterday, Boot."

His eyes narrow, and I know he doesn't believe me. I probably don't believe myself.

Mr. Maddox says, "Does that work for you, Boot?"

"I guess." He doesn't mean it.

"Okay, we'll start again," he says. "What game do you want to play? Boot, you choose this time."

He looks at the stack of board games. "Connect Four."

"Okay," he says. "Let's get it out and go over the rules."

"I know how to play," Boot says. "You try to get four in a row, like tic-tac-toe."

I tell him I know the game, too.

"Okay," he says. "I'll ask Mrs. Taylor to remind you when it's time to go down to lunch."

He gets up and goes to the door. "This room is drafty. Are you comfortable in here?"

"I'm fine," I say.

"Boot?"

He doesn't respond.

"Boot?" I say in a loud voice.

He jerks his head up to look at me.

"Mr. Maddox wants to know if you're warm enough."

He turns and looks surprised to see Maddox still standing in the doorway. "Yeah," he says.

Mr. Maddox nods and disappears from the doorway.

I look at Boot. I remember what happened when I corrected his pronunciation of authors' names yesterday. I thought he was mad and ignoring me, but that wasn't it at all. He didn't hear me.

Boot has a hearing problem.

I pull off my shoes and kick them to the side. "Don't tell me if my feet smell."

He grimaces. "They stink."

"No, they don't. I used foot powder this morning. I know for a fact that they don't stink." I smile at him, but he glares back. I set up the Connect Four frame on the coffee table as he watches. I slide the box over to him. "Why don't you divide up the checkers."

He doesn't ask whether I want black or red; he gathers up the reds and slides them over to me.

"You go first," I tell him. I speak up a little to be sure he hears. "I went first last time."

He looks surprised that I let him go first. He picks up a black checker and drops it into the middle slot.

I'm ready with my first red one and drop it into the slot to the right of his checker. He stares at the two checkers for nearly a minute before he follows with a black one to the left of his first checker. He now has two in a row, so I drop my red next to them.

We continue playing for a while. Boot's a slow player, and I get bored waiting for him. He studies the checkers for at least a full minute before each of his plays. I'm getting hungry, so I take out a roll of Life Savers from my pocket, pull out a red one, and pop it into my mouth. Boot looks up at me.

"Cherry—my favorite," I say. "Yum." He scowls. "Come on, Boot. It's your turn."

"I *know*," he says. "Bug off."

I roll my eyes and sigh loudly. I hope he hears. "Tick, tick, tick," I say.

He scowls again. "Shut up." Then he looks up at me. "Anyway, we have to stay here for two hours. What do you care how fast we play?"

"I'm bored," I tell him.

"Too bad," he says and begins studying the checkers in the frame again.

I hear his stomach growl. It's so loud, I wonder if Mr. Maddox can hear it in his office.

"Look," I say. "If you make your move now, I'll give you a Life Saver." I hold up the roll.

He looks at me again, and I can tell he wants one. I can almost hear him salivating. He swallows. His stomach growls again. I smile.

"Make your move," I say. I take out a yellow Life Saver and wiggle it in front of his face. "Doesn't this look *good*? If you make your move in five seconds, it's yours, okay? One, two . . ."

"Don't rush me," he says.

"Boot, this is a game of Connect Four. We're not negotiating world peace. Three . . ."

"Shut up. I'm thinking."

"Four." I pause. "Come on. Four and a half." Pause. I roll my eyes. "Four and three quarters." I sigh. "Don't you want a Life Saver?"

Slowly, he picks up a checker.

"All right," I say, and I think he's going to drop it in a slot, but he freezes with his hand over the slot to think some more.

"Four and seven eighths." *Why can't he just drop it into the slot?* "Five." He drops the checker on top of one of his other checkers two seconds after I say it.

He extends his hand toward me, palm up. "Give it to me."

"That was a *lot* longer than five seconds," I say. He looks really mad. "Boot, the deal was that you were supposed to *hurry up* to get a Life Saver. But you took even longer than usual."

"Lardbutt."

"If you're not careful, I'm going to start liking that nickname," I say. "But maybe you meant it as a term of endearment." He doesn't speak. He stares at the Connect Four frame. "How's your hand?"

His head snaps up, suspicion blazing in his eyes. I don't want him to think I'm being sarcastic, so I say, "You smashed it into the wall so hard, I thought you'd be wearing a cast today."

"What's it to you?"

I shrug. "Nothing. You must be the most stoic person I've ever met."

"Yeah?" he said through his teeth. "Well, *you're* a lardbutt, which is a lot worse. And you better get used to me calling you lardbutt, because that's what you are, you fat slob."

"I just gave you a compliment, Boot," I say. "You took all that pain without screaming."

His face looks sour, and he stares away. I say, "Okay, it's my turn." I pick up a red checker and drop it into the slot on top of his two stacked black ones. "Now it's yours."

Probably two minutes later, he's still staring at the frame. "Geez," I say and lie down on the couch. "Wake me up when it's my turn." I close my eyes and fold my arms over my chest.

CHAPTER NINE

Boot's Turn

T ELEVEN FORTY-THREE, the bell rings, so it's time for lunch. I've been real hungry and was keeping a close watch on the clock.

Mick had been pretending to sleep between plays while he waited for me to move, so I'd have to say, "Your turn," every time. He'd snort and flick his eyes open and closed as if I'd startled him from a deep sleep.

I get up and head for the door. Mrs. Taylor is busy at her desk. She forgot to tell us it was lunchtime, so I just leave, and I know she sees me. I don't turn around to see if Mick is following me or if he's still pretending to sleep and didn't hear me leave. I'm half-starved, but I don't want to end up in the caf line right in front of him, so I stop in the bathroom before going downstairs.

J.K.'s in here. "You play games today?" he asks.

"Not much," I say. I remember the bruise on my arm from last night where it hit the edge of the stove, and I show it to him.

"Sullivan did that?" he asks.

"Yeah, but I gave as good as I got."

He smiles. "I can't believe the new principal wants you to play games," he says. "What's his name?"

I shrug. "I don't know. Something. I can't remember."

He waits for me, and we walk down to the caf.

"Too bad you can't sit at our table," he says. "I want to hear about that fight."

I shrug like it was no big deal. "I'll tell you later."

We go through the line and pick up our food. I see some of the kids are turning around in the lunch line, looking at me. Some others are watching from their tables. They look at me and put their heads together, talking and grinning. One guy, Rodney Phillips, the quarterback of our football team, nods and gives me sort of a smile. I nod back, and I feel myself stand a little straighter.

"Okay, well . . . later, man," J.K. says after we've got our lunches. "See you after the game room."

"Yeah, see ya." I walk alone to the caf door feeling everybody's eyes on me. I see Tabitha sitting at her regular table with her friends. I wink at her, and her eyes get huge. She covers her mouth with her hand, while her friends lean in and make screamy noises.

Man. This is unbelievable. I walk toward the principal's office, and I feel like I'm kind of in a dream. I wish this game-room thing would go on forever.

Only without Sullivan.

He's already there when I get back to the game room. His lunch is on the coffee table. He's sitting cross-legged on the floor between the coffee table and the couch. His shoes are off and under the table.

"Sloppy joes," he says. He holds his up with two hands.

"Duh," I say. I know if Tabitha was here, she'd laugh. I smile to myself.

I set my tray on the end of the table. Sullivan's moved the Connect Four frame to the floor, and I look to see if he cheated by rearranging the checkers while I was gone, but he didn't. I sit on my chair.

I'm real hungry, so I dive into my lunch. Sloppy joes, peaches, green beans, a cookie, and a carton of chocolate milk. Not too bad. I eat it all in about three minutes. I look up and Sullivan's staring at me.

"What?" I say.

"Do you always inhale food like that?"

I frown. "What do you mean?" It's got to be a trick question.

"I mean, you nailed that food in record time. Didn't you eat breakfast this morning?"

That makes me mad. "What's it to you?"

He shrugs. "Forget it."

I pick up his cookie and throw it across the room. It lands next to the desk that's pushed up against the far wall. He looks at me as if I'm nuts, so I smile. "Go get it," I tell him.

He shakes his head, and he's so big, it takes him five minutes to get up off the floor. I get this idea all of a sudden, and while he walks across the room to get the cookie, I scoop up some of his peaches and dump them into his shoe. I add a spoonful of juice before he finds the cookie and picks it up.

He comes back, and I try to keep the smile off my face. I start thinking how I'm going to tell Tabitha about this. *"Yeah, you should've heard Sullivan yell. It was great."*

He sits down on the floor again and picks a clump of dust off the cookie. He makes a face. "There's dirt on it." He brushes it on his shirt and looks at it again, then throws it on my tray. "Thanks a lot."

"Any time," I say.

He still has a few bites of hamburger bun, so he eats it and sets his tray on the floor next to his shoes. He looks at the clock on the wall. "We only have five more minutes before the bell."

"Seven," I say. He looks at me, and I say, "We have seven more minutes."

"Have it your way, Boot. Seven. We might as well finish the game."

I put my lunch tray on the floor, and he moves the Connect Four frame back to the table.

"We've both won three games," he says. "I figured out your strategy, Quinn. You move as slow as a glacier, so I get bored and stop paying attention."

I'm still feeling great about my wink that made Tabitha and her friends crazy, so I say, "Or maybe I'm a good player, and you're dumber than you think."

He looks up at the ceiling like he's thinking that over. "Nah," he finally says. "Couldn't be that."

Just wait till you put your shoes on, I say to myself.

"So who's turn is it?" he asks.

I don't remember, so I tell him, "Mine."

"Go ahead. Think you can make a move before the bell rings?"

I ignore him and look at the frame. He takes the roll of Life Savers out of his pocket, fingers out a green one, and pops it into his mouth. He sees me watching. "You want a Life Saver?"

I figure it's a trick question, but I say, "Yeah."

So he takes the one out of his mouth and holds it in his hand. "Here, you can have mine." I glare at him. He shrugs and pops it back in his mouth. "Ingrate. I'm so nice to you. And after you threw away my cookie, too."

Ring, bell.

"So make a move, why don't you?" he says.

I see something I hadn't seen before. I pick up a checker and drop it into a slot. "You're dead now, Sullivan."

He looks at the frame and goes, "Oh, man!" and I laugh because I got him in a trap. If he drops his checker on the left side, I can get a row of a diagonal four on the right. And if he drops his checker to block that one, I have a row of three overhead just begging for me to add a fourth on the end for a win.

"I can't believe I missed that!" he says and drops his checker in the frame.

"You're not as smart as you think you are, brainiac." Let him think I set up the trap on purpose. I drop the checker to get the diagonal four. I'd be more excited about the win if I wasn't thinking about what was about to happen.

He reaches for his shoes, and I hold my breath.

He puts on his right shoe first, which doesn't have the peach. I push the lever that releases the checkers from the frame, and then I start scooping them up to put them away in the box. But all the time, I'm watching out the corner of my eye.

He picks up his left shoe and shoves his foot in. His eyes get big and surprised, and his mouth opens wide, and he lets out a yell from deep in his throat.

I stand up and laugh and clap, and I do this dance like a star quarterback that's just scored a touchdown.

He takes his foot out of his shoe, and there's little pieces of mashed peach still stuck on his sock that's dripping with peach juice. I can hardly stand it, I'm laughing so hard.

He looks in his shoe and makes a face when he sees what's in there, and he dumps the peaches and juice onto his lunch tray. I wait to see if he comes after me. I'm ready for him, even though I'm still laughing.

But he doesn't come after me. In fact, he doesn't even move. He just shakes his head with this smile on his face. And then he holds up his pointer finger, and smiles.

"You got me good, Boot," he says. "But you probably know—this means war."

That surprises me, and I say, "This always *was* a war."

He just stares at me. When he talks again, this is what he says: "I guess you're right about that, Boot. It always *was* a war."

CHAPTER TEN

Mick's Turn

BOOT REALLY GOT me with that peach trick. I have to say, he did a good job the way he pulled it off. His timing was perfect, throwing the cookie to get me away from my shoes just long enough. So it turns out Boot's a wily guy, which is really surprising.

He said this always was a war, and, for some reason, it wasn't until he said it that I realized how seriously he takes all this stuff between us. I mean, I knew he hated me, but I thought we were both kind of enjoying the *game* of hating each other. And maybe he is. I'm sure he got a kick out of his victory with the peaches.

Anyway, I go around school for the rest of the day with a wet sock inside my shoe, and I can feel my toes sticking together.

Some of the kids are looking at me and grinning. "Hey,

Mick!" someone calls out. "I heard what happened in the game room."

"I always wondered what stepping into peaches would feel like," I say. "And let me tell you—it was better than I imagined."

And they laugh.

After school, I'm walking out the front door, and I see Tabitha. Right away she says, "I heard what happened today."

I wonder how long it took Boot to give her his good news personally. Then I realize that part of the war we're fighting is over Tabitha: to impress her, to get her to like one of us over the other. I wonder if girls know how crazy we can get over them. I mean, guys have this primitive thing going on in our heads. Boot and I are acting like two lions, or roosters, or even cavemen fighting over a female. You'd think that modern humans—in a supposedly civilized society—would be above all that. But we're not. It's amazing, really.

Anyway, Tabitha's smiling up at me. "How's your foot feeling?"

"Just peachy," I say, and she lets out one of her great laughs.

"You should've heard Boot telling everybody about it in language arts class," she says. "Everybody was going nuts."

Unfortunately, I can picture it.

She keeps smiling, and I'm wondering what kissing a girl with braces is like. Actually, I don't even know what kissing a girl *without* braces is like, so it's pretty hard to imagine a soft mouth with those bands behind it.

She says, "Hey, I'm going to walk down to the Corner and get a Coke. Want to come?"

Tabitha's asking me to walk with her? It seems too good to be true, so I'm not sure I heard right.

"What?" I lean in, hoping she'll say what I thought she said.

She laughs and cups her hands around her mouth and yells, *"Want a so-da at the Cor-ner? That's where I'm go-ing!"*

I laugh and feel my blood rushing through my veins. "Sure," I say.

So we head down the sidewalk away from school, and it feels great walking next to her. She's swinging her hips as usual, and I try not to think about it, because if I do, I'll go crazy.

"So is Boot any good at playing games?" she asks.

I think about that for a second. I can either be honest, or I can make him look bad. "He's lousy," I say. She lets out another laugh, but I feel a tiny bit guilty, so I say, "Actually, he's not as dumb as he looks." That feels something like a compromise, and she laughs even more.

I think this might be the best day of my life. Even peaches in my shoe is a small price to pay to be here, walking with Tabitha. I look around, wondering if anyone is noticing that I—Mick Sullivan, who can't catch a fly ball; or score a touchdown; or run down the court, gracefully dribbling a basketball—am walking down the street with every guy's fantasy, Tabitha Slater. *Am I dreaming?*

"Hey, lardbutt!"

Of course. He wasn't happy just beating me at Connect Four and pouring peaches in my shoe. Now he has to horn in on my walk with Tabitha.

Tabitha giggles. "Uh-oh."

We're outside the Corner now, and the door opens. Her two friends, Abby and Cheyanne, walk out. They see Tabitha with me, and they look over and see Boot, who's trudging up the sidewalk with Jerrod and Clay, and they say, "Ooo! This is going to be good!"

Everybody gathers around us, waiting to see what happens.

I guess I'm going to have to play my part, so I wait to see how Boot handles it. I realize that this is the second time in one day that Boot and I have faced off in front of people who're having a good time with it. I can see that Boot is watching the crowd of people assembling, too, and he's looking a little bit nervous.

So I say, "Boot, why don't we just agree that we hate each other and go our way?"

Of course, part of my attention is on Tabitha. I notice a look of disappointment that flits across her face. It surprises me that she's bloodthirsty, but girls always surprise me, so that's nothing new.

Boot, who knows he can always fall back on Jerrod and Clay, says, "Are you going to run away again like a scared . . ." He falters.

I know he can't remember the animal, so I say, "Like a scared what, Boot?"

Boot glances at Jerrod and Clay, who look away because they can't remember it, either.

"Rabbit," he says.

"Nope," I say. "Or even a scared gazelle." After all, Tabitha is here. I can't very well do my imitation of a leaping ballet dancer. I stare hard at Boot, trying to read his mind. He's bound to be thinking about Tabitha, too. The stakes are astronomically high for both of us.

Then she really surprises me. She steps over and puts a hand on my arm. "Don't fight," Tabitha says. "I don't want anyone to get hurt."

As far as Boot is concerned, that isn't the right thing to say. Or do. (I mean, the touching me thing.) Boot must think she's worried that I'll beat him up—and he doesn't want her to think he's a sissy—because he comes over, gently moves her aside, and hits me in the mouth with his fist.

The kids all start hollering, and I stagger back a few steps. I put my hand to my lip, and it comes back bloody.

"*Oh, Mike!*" Tabitha yells.

"Mick," someone says.

"Oh, yeah," she says. "*Oh, Mick!*"

She still doesn't remember my name?

That startles the anger right out of me, so I don't come running at Boot. It gives me a second to clear my head.

I like taunting Boot, but I know I can really hurt him because I'm so much bigger, and except for when he insulted my dad, I've never really wanted to kill him or do serious damage. Usually I taunt him till he hits me. I might box his ears to show him I'm not a total wuss, but I never hurt him too much.

On the other hand, my lip is bleeding and Tabitha's standing here—even though she hasn't gotten my name down yet—so I go flying at him. I knock him over, and we slug it out on the grass. (I'm smart enough to run at him from an angle, so we don't land on the concrete.)

After a while, I'm pulled off Boot. It turns out to be Adam and Connor, who have materialized magically without my knowing it.

"Hey, that's enough," Adam says. "Don't kill him, Mick."

I glance at Tabitha, who's looking at me, her eyes shining. Adam and Connor hold me back, and I see that Boot's getting to his feet. He has that ferocious look that comes out of humiliation.

And I know that even if I stop harassing him, we haven't had our last fight.

I let Adam and Connor lead me off down the street.

I wish Tabitha and I could've had that soda, but seeing

that look in her eyes is even better. I'm leaving on a high note, with her wanting more of me.

I get home and wash the blood off my mouth. The phone rings, so I go to answer it. I'm still on a high from that look in Tabitha's eyes, and I say "hello," hoping this is fast. Any conversation wouldn't be as much fun as thinking about Tabitha.

So when she says, "Hey, Mick," I don't even know who it is. If she'd said, "Hey, *Mike*," I'd know for sure, but she got it right this time.

So I say something stupid like "Uh-hunh?"

"This is Tabitha."

This time it's a rocket that blasts off in my chest. "Hi," I say.

"We didn't get those sodas."

"Yeah, sorry." Even though I haven't just run a race, I'm breathless.

"Want to meet me?"

"Sure."

"I'll be under the Twelfth Avenue Bridge in a half hour," she says. "I'll bring Cokes."

"Okay," I say.

Part of me is standing outside of myself watching my whole body shake. I can't believe I'm feeling like this. Here's this girl on the phone, and I'm scared out of my wits. Really, this isn't me. On the other hand, I hardly ever talk to girls, unless it's to say something like, "Can I borrow a pencil?" so I really haven't gotten to know the *me* who talks to girls.

"See you." She hangs up.

I stand there, blinking. *What do I do now?* I mean, is there a standard procedure for getting ready to meet a girl? I suppose I could brush my teeth and comb my hair. Maybe wash my hands. My left foot is still sticky, so I want to wash it and put on a different pair of shoes.

I clean myself up and then pace around the house for fifteen minutes, getting sweaty from nerves. After the time is up, I head over to the bridge.

The Twelfth Avenue Bridge has always been a meeting place because it's practically in the center of town where the river divides the town in half. It's fairly quiet there, too, unless a lot of traffic happens to be roaring across it.

The people from my school live on the north side of the river. I think everybody secretly wishes they could live on the south side, where the nicer houses are, but I don't know anyone who would admit it. There's a kind of fierce loyalty that we northerners have, especially at high-school basketball games. The southern kids think they're better than we are, and they yell mean things at us. Of course, it's entirely possible that some of our kids yell first. But who keeps track?

I don't mind admitting that I want a better life than my dad's. I'm just quiet about who I say that to. Mom understands, and she tells me to keep reading, that education is my ticket out of the north side. And out of town. After high school, believe me, I'm walking out of here, and I'm never looking back.

Except maybe I'll look back at today. I think I just might remember meeting Tabitha under the bridge.

When I get there, she's sitting on a low, flat rock, throwing pebbles into the water.

"Hey," I say, over the thunder booming in my chest.

She looks up and smiles. "Hey, Mick."

I couldn't help noticing that she's gotten my name right twice in the last half hour. The day is getting better and better.

She pulls a paper bag off the ground, reaches in, and pulls out a can of Coke. "Here," she says. She hands it to me. Her fingers brush against mine, and I wonder if she notices. She opens another can for herself.

She smiles. "Boot sure hates you."

"Yeah." I sit down on the gravel next to her rock. I'm big enough, though, that we're almost on the same level. "It's one of his special talents."

She laughs. "And your talent is hating *him*?"

"No, I don't hate him," I say. "But it's fun making him miserable sometimes."

"Everybody's talking about you guys," she says. "They

want to hear all about the game room and your fights."

I don't want to waste valuable conversation time with Tabitha talking about Boot—and besides, I want to get to know her—so I say, "So what do you do for fun?"

She seems surprised by the question. "Oh, I like to hang out with my friends, mostly. Listen to music on the radio. How about you? I mean, besides making Boot miserable?"

I don't know if I should say it, but she seems interested, so I tell her the truth. "I like to read."

"Really?" She runs a hand through her hair. "I read magazines sometimes."

"I do, too, but mostly I read books."

"You mean, like from the library?"

"Yeah. The library's kind of my home away from home. I spend a lot of time there."

"Hunh." She gazes off. Then she does something totally unexpected.

She turns, leans in, and kisses me. Right on the mouth.

I'm so surprised, I just stare at her. Then it occurs to me that I can kiss her back. Duh. So I do.

Just for the record, kissing a girl with braces is really great; I can't even tell. Then I realize that her kisses taste like peanut butter. She must have had a snack before coming here. I'm not complaining, though; peanut butter is one of my favorite flavors.

We kiss for a while, and I think maybe kissing is my new

favorite thing to do; it's even better than reading. I hold her face in my hand while we kiss, and her cheek is cool and smooth.

Then she pulls away, smiling, and says, "Well, see you at school tomorrow."

"Uh . . ." I don't want her to go. "Do you have to leave right now?"

"Yeah, I should." She checks her watch. "I've got to get home. I told Cheyanne I'd call her before supper and go over math problems."

I wonder if she'll tell Cheyanne about the kissing.

"Okay," I say. She gets up. "That's very nice of you."

She frowns. "What's nice of me?"

"I mean, going over math problems with Cheyanne." *Did she think I meant she was nice to kiss me?*

"Oh." She shrugs and smiles. "No big deal. Well, see ya. Say hi to Boot tomorrow in the game room."

That stops me short. Does she seriously think I'm going to say hi to my rival for her? But then I realize it: Boot and I aren't rivals anymore—at least not where Tabitha is concerned. That's because she's chosen *me*.

I might've floated home, but I don't know, because I don't remember anything between Tabitha leaving me at the river and arriving home a while later. I play some music on the CD player in my room and stare out the window till dinner. And just a fact for the record: I've never done that before. It occurs to me that I'm doing a lot of things I've never done before.

After Dad gets home, we all sit at the dining room table. The phone rings, and he gets up and answers it. Mom and I are both watching him. His face darkens. He doesn't say anything for about a minute while he listens to whoever is on the line. His face doesn't give us any clues.

Finally, he says, "Okay. You had your say. Are you through?" The person must have said "yes." "Okay. I'll meet with you tomorrow after work. At Jamboree."

Mom and I look at each other. Jamboree is a restaurant, but they also have a bar. On the rare occasions that we go out to eat, Mom and I try to steer clear of places that serve drinks other than water, coffee, and soda. There's no reason to tempt him.

Dad hangs up the phone. "You'll never guess who that was," he says.

"Who?" Mom and I ask together.

"Dave."

"Dave," Mom says, thinking. "Oh, your brother?"

"Yeah," he says. "After all these years, he wants to get together again. Says he's in AA, and he's supposed to, you know, make amends with people."

I dimly remember Uncle Dave. He and Dad had a falling out when I was about seven, and until now, they haven't spoken.

"Honey, that's wonderful," Mom says.

Dad stares into space and nods. "Says he's doing well. He's not married to Melanie anymore. Got divorced, and now he's married to a woman named Rita." He looks at Mom. "How about that . . . I would never have believed this could happen."

Mom's face takes on a hopeful look. "Wouldn't it be wonderful to have your brother in your life again?"

"We'll see how it goes."

"You're seeing him tomorrow?" Mom asks.

"Yeah."

I hope it'll go well. For everybody's sake.

Through dinner, Dad's mood gets better and better. Maybe he's thinking about his brother and maybe not. He doesn't say.

After dinner, he stands up and says to me, "How about we see if you can take me this time?"

Inside, I groan. Another arm-wrestling match. He hasn't challenged me for about six months, and I'd hoped he'd forgotten about it.

"I have homework, Dad," I say. I glance at Mom who's gathering up dishes from the table. She avoids looking at me.

He rolls his eyes. "How long does it take to arm wrestle? Come on—I don't want to hear excuses."

I sigh. "Just one time, okay?"

He slides his plate to the side and sets his elbow on the

table. "Come on," he says. His eyes are gleaming.

I put my elbow on the table and grasp his hand.

"Ready? Let's go," he says, and his arm muscles clench as he begins to move my arm till he pushes it back at a seventy-degree angle. "You've got to build yourself up," he tells me. "You're big, but you need to be strong, too, if you want people to respect you."

At first, I had resisted a little bit, but now I gather my strength and begin to move his arm back till our hands are gripped at the top of the arc. I don't want to hear any more from him that I'm not strong enough or that people won't respect me if I'm not macho enough. And slowly, I push his arm backward till our clasped hands are about three inches from his side of the table.

Then I see the look on his face. He's straining like crazy, and he looks scared. I think he's panicked that I could be stronger than he is. He knows that I don't even work out, and that would mean that he's not as strong as he used to be.

So I can't do it. The arm-wrestling match is too important to him.

I relax just a little bit, and he pushes my hand to the table in less than a minute. Relief washes over his face. He stands and hitches up his pants. "You're getting stronger, boy. But not strong enough."

"You're right, Dad," I say. "You're stronger than I'll ever be."

He seems happy. I watch him walk out of the dining

room, and I feel this weird sadness. He disappears around the corner, and I realize that I didn't *want* to find out that I'm stronger than he is.

I look over and see Mom. I didn't know she was still in the room, but she nods to me, and I know that *she* knows I threw the contest.

She walks past me and gives my shoulder a squeeze. "You're a good guy, Mick," she murmurs.

CHAPTER ELEVEN

Boot's Turn

I FIGURED THE PEACH trick would get me points with Tabitha. She sure laughed when I told everybody about it in language arts class. So when I saw her walking with Sullivan after school, I could hardly believe it.

And when she went over and touched Mick and said she didn't want anybody to get hurt, I figured she was saying that I'm not strong enough to defend myself. So I had to show her I *could* fight Sullivan.

And I did, too. I gave as good as I got before those guys hauled him off me.

But when the fight was over, Tabitha was looking at Mick like he was her hero or something, and that made me hate him even more. If I could shove him down an empty elevator shaft, I'd do it.

I go home, turn up the music in my headphones, and try to blast the face of Tabitha Slater out of my mind.

I don't realize that Dad's home till he comes down and turns off the music. I jump a little because my eyes are closed. I didn't know he'd opened the door to my room.

"Come on up," he says. "I got us a pizza."

I'm glad he isn't mad. Sometimes when I'm listening to music and I can't hear him, he tells me he's been yelling at the top of the basement stairs for ten minutes. At least he doesn't throw water on me when I'm listening to music. Maybe he thinks he'll electrocute me because I'm attached to the CD player.

I get up and follow him upstairs. Dad empties the change and a few bills from his pocket into the cookie jar on the counter. Ethan's home, sitting on the couch in front of the TV.

Dad puts the pizza on a TV tray in the living room. Then he mutes the TV, sits on the couch, and says, "Well, guys, I've got good news."

I sit on the edge of the red chair. I can't remember Dad ever saying he has good news, so I'm paying attention.

"Cliff called me into his office today, and I got a promotion. You're looking at the new store manager at Mailing Plus. I get a seven thousand dollar raise, and it'll go up from there, too."

Ethan and I whoop and say congratulations. I can't

remember ever seeing him look this happy.

"Maybe we can get a car," I say. Our old Chevy's got over two hundred thousand miles on it, and it's rusty and breaks down all the time.

Dad turns to me. "Yeah," he says. "That's what I was thinking."

Ethan starts talking about what kind of car we should get. He wants us to get a sports car, maybe a Porsche, but Dad says, "Whatever it is, it'll be an *American* car. And a brand-new one." We've never bought a new car before, so that'll be really cool.

We start eating and end up watching a movie on cable. It's about a guy who gets a job working for the Mafia, and lots of people get killed, only he doesn't care until his brother is murdered. And then he wants out. Almost everybody dies in the end, except for the main guy in the story. So you're glad they all die, because now he can get out of the Mob and go straight.

After the movie, I decide to walk over to River City Music in case Jesse's there. It's a nice night, and it's almost dark out. I can't help thinking about Tabitha and wishing she was my girlfriend and I was walking with her right now. But that makes me feel bad, so I try to think of something else, and I hum a song I heard on the radio the other day. I wonder why Tabitha suddenly acts like she likes Mick better than me. Everybody was talking today at school about how I pulled a fast one on Mick with the peaches. They were all laughing about it and congratulating me. But after school at the Corner, she glommed on to Mick when I was standing right there.

But I don't want to think about it, so I push it out of my mind. I don't need her anyways.

I can see River City Music a half a block away, and it's dark inside, so I don't think anyone is there. But when I'm just outside it, I look through the front window and see what I think is the flash of a tiny light inside. It snaps out right away. I go to the glass and cover the sides of my face to get a better look inside.

That's when I see a shadow move. I know it's not Jesse because even if he's in the back, he'd turn on one of the fluorescents overhead.

I walk to the alley behind the store. It's pretty dark because the only light here is the one on the back of a lamp store a few buildings away. But I get to River City's back door, and I see it's been jimmied open. Someone's broke in, I know, and I panic for a second before my mind settles down and tells me I better call the cops.

This would be a great time for a cell phone, but I don't have one, so I run to the door a little ways down that leads to the apartment of the guy who called the cops on Jesse that time he was playing his music too loud.

I run up the creaky stairs and under this bare lightbulb

screwed into the ceiling. I bang on his door. Pretty soon this old guy opens the door, and I tell him that River City Music is getting robbed. He doesn't say anything. He just stands there with his mouth opening and closing like a fish. So I say, "Can I call the cops?" and he says "yes," and steps to the side. So I run inside and find the phone—the old guy points out where it is—and I dial nine one one.

I tell the operator there's a burglary going on at River City Music. She says she'll call the police but I should stay where I'm safe.

But I don't want to stay with the old man, so after I put the phone down, I head for the door.

"If someone's robbin' the place, you better not go downstairs yet," the old guy says. "It might be dangerous."

But I sort of just wave at him and leave. I don't plan to stop the burglar or do anything risky. But I don't want him to get away with money or instruments from the store. If I can get a look at him, maybe I can tell the cops what he looks like. I know River City Music does okay, but twice Jesse told me that his dad was worried because a new, bigger music store across town was taking away a lot of business.

So I walk real quiet down the stairs, open the door a crack, and look into the alley. I don't see anyone, so I take a step outside, and I'm careful closing the door. Then I walk slow over to River City's back door.

I don't stand there more than half a minute while my eyes are trying to adjust to the dark, when the door opens and out comes this big guy. Part of me is scared, but I remember I've got to memorize his face, so I freeze where I am.

And he turns and plows right into me, knocks me over backward, and he runs off down the alley. I get up just in time to see a police car charging into the alley right in front of him. It blocks him, so he turns and runs back toward me. He's really big, and I start to move out of his way, and then I realize I can help, so I tackle him. Right there in the alley. He goes down hard, and starts to kick me.

The cops are there in a couple of seconds, pulling him up to his feet, and slapping the cuffs on his wrists. I walk back to the squad car with them. They read him his rights like they do on TV, put him in the backseat, and turn to me. They start in with the questions: was I the guy who called them? How did I know a robbery was in progress? What's my name and address, and all that.

One of the cops even gives me a ride home. I wonder if the neighbors see the squad car pull up in front of my house.

Before I get out of the car, the cop goes, "You know I should tell you that what you did was dangerous—tackling the perp like that—and you shouldn't have done it." I nod. Then he grins and puts his hand out. "But I gotta say it, you're a brave kid. Thanks for the help."

I shake his hand, get out of the car, and walk up to my house. I realize I have this big, stupid grin on my face, and I wipe it off when I get to the door. But I can't wait to tell Dad and Ethan what I did.

CHAPTER TWELVE

Mick's Turn

DURING MY WALK to school, I think about Tabitha kissing me. And that leads to thinking about kissing her back. I wonder if she'll tell her friends about it. I don't know much about girls, but from what I've observed at school, it seems as if they do a lot of talking about themselves.

So I figure she'll tell her friends. And those friends, if they're interested enough and it's a slow gossip day at school, will tell other friends. And pretty soon, everyone will know that Tabitha and I are going out.

I could live with that.

I don't see her when I get to school, but the airfield in my chest is roaring with all the jets taking off and landing. I'm so nervous and jittery that a couple of times I actually hope that I *don't* see her. And then I realize how ridiculous that is. Of *course* I want to see her! If I don't see her today, I'll go crazy. So should I look her in the eyes when I talk to her? Should I act happy to see her or play it cool? I wish someone would write a book and spell out the best way to act in situations like this, so people wouldn't have to bungle their way through a first boy-girl relationship.

I wonder if Tabitha is used to boy-girl relationships. She must have kissed other boys before yesterday. She sure is good at it. Maybe she's kissed *lots* of boys, and that's how she perfected her technique. I'm a strong believer in education, so if she wants to teach me the nuances of great kissing, I wouldn't try to stop her.

All during the morning, I'm scanning the halls for her. I don't see her, and just before going to the game room, I have a terrible feeling: what if she's sick today and doesn't come to school? And what if I have to wait a whole day to see her again? Or two whole days? What if we exchanged germs when we were kissing yesterday, and I come down with the flu that she has now, just as she's getting better, and then *I* get sick and have to be out of school for a whole week?

It would actually be kind of cool if everybody knew that Tabitha Slater gave me the flu. That would be the only comfort I'd have while I'm lying in bed with a fever or barfing my brains out.

I turn the corner near the game room, and there she is, standing at her locker with Cheyanne.

The air-traffic controller gives a signal and every jet in my chest roars into the sky in a massive spectacle of figure eights and loop-de-loops. For a second, I wonder if I'm having a heart attack.

She turns and sees me and smiles. "Hey, Mick," she calls out in a singsongy kind of voice. She turns and giggles in Cheyanne's direction. Cheyanne's eyes get big. She grins back and gives Tabitha a little playful jab on the arm.

Okay, I don't claim to be fluent in female body language, but I'd be willing to bet that a rough translation of what I just saw might include a reference to yesterday's kissing under the bridge.

I realize I'm not breathing, so I order myself to take in some air, which keeps the jets aloft. "Hey," I manage to say on the exhale.

She bangs her locker shut and walks over with Cheyanne close behind. "You're going to the game room now, hunh?" she says.

"Yeah." My brain searches for something else to say, but once again, she's rendered me speechless.

Then two things happen together that I couldn't have planned and timed any better: 1) Tabitha comes over and takes hold of my hand, and 2) Boot rounds the corner and sees us. His face collapses, he seems to shrink about an inch, and his shoulders droop.

Tabitha flashes a smile at him and says, "Hi, Boot. Should I stand in between you guys and referee?" Cheyanne, right behind her, laughs.

Boot surprises me by drawing himself back up and planting a smile on his face. "If you read something in the papers about a robbery over at River City Music, don't be surprised."

"Why?" I ask him. "You rob the place?"

Of course, I know that whatever he's about to say is for Tabitha's benefit, but I have to admit I'm curious, too, even though it's hard to focus on anything other than Tabitha's little hand—cool and dry—in mine.

"No, lardbutt," he says. "I stopped the robbery and caught the perp."

"'The *perp*?'" I say. "What gives me the impression that you've been watching too much TV?"

But he's gotten Tabitha's attention, and she slips her hand loose and moves toward him, an eager look in her eyes. "You caught the perp? Really? How'd you do *that*?"

Now I'm starting to get nervous. I know he's lying, but apparently Tabitha doesn't suspect.

"Tackled him," Boot says. He's underplaying it, looking slightly bored with the telling. But his eyes are sharp and focused on Tabitha. "I called the cops after I saw him inside, and when he ran out into the alley, I tackled him and held him till the cops got there."

"You *did*?"

Geez. She's buying it. Cheyanne, too. She comes up and stands next to Tabitha, her mouth slightly open.

"You could've gotten hurt," Tabitha says. She looks impressed.

"Did you first hear about the robbery on the radio this morning, Boot?" I ask him.

He scowls briefly but doesn't bother to look at me. He aims this directly at Tabitha: "One of the cops gave me a ride home in the squad car and said I was brave and thanked me for the help. And the owner of the store and his son called this morning to say they were grateful for what I did."

"That's so cool, Boot!" Tabitha says, while Cheyanne makes noises to indicate how impressed she is. "Maybe you'll get a hero award or something."

"Maybe." He gives her a smile, and she beams one back at him.

Great.

"Well," he says. "I guess I better get to the game room."

"You're so conscientious, Boot," I say. That sounds petty, but it slipped out before I could stop it.

Boot ambles off down the hall.

"He might've really stopped the robbery, you know," Tabitha says. She grins. "You just don't like him and don't want to believe it."

I say, "Maybe you're right," on the off chance that there's a little bit of truth in what he said. After all, maybe he was nearby and saw the police cars in the area, then heard about the robbery on the radio.

I know the bell is about to ring. "See you after school?" I ask her.

"Okay," she says.

"I'll meet you at your locker."

"Yeah. See ya." She and Cheyanne hurry away, their heads together, whispering. I have a rotten feeling they're talking about Boot, the hero.

I walk into the principal's office, and Mrs. Taylor gestures for me to go on back to the game room. It's weird that I can be totally happy one minute, then Tabitha drops my hand and looks impressed with Boot, and I'm instantly sure that I'm losing her. And we haven't even been boyfriend and girlfriend for a whole day yet. It's amazing the power girls have.

Boot's sitting on the couch when I walk in.

I take the big chair on the other side of the coffee table. I don't want him to know I'm worried about Tabitha. "Hey, Boot."

He looks up at me. "Maybe I'll get mentioned in the paper tomorrow."

"You want to play Battleship?" I ask him.

"You don't have to believe that I stopped the robbery."

"Well, that's good, Boot," I say, "because I don't. So,

you want to play Battleship?"

"Because whether you believe it or not, it happened."

"Okay. Battleship it is."

I pull the box from the pile of games on the table and move the others to the floor. I open it and put one of the plastic kits in front of him. He doesn't move. I open my kit and start to set up my ships.

He peers over at me then and murmurs, "Tabitha and Cheyanne believed me."

I ignore that. "You better get your ships in place. I'm about to start the game."

"I don't *care* if you don't believe me."

"You said that," I say. "So let's play. You know how to play this one?"

"Duh," he says.

But just to make sure, I say, "Your vertical target grid represents my horizontal ocean grid. You try to hit each of my ships the number of times required to sink it."

"I said I know how to play," he tells me. He opens his plastic kit.

I like to put the smallest ship, the destroyer, along one edge of the ocean grid, so it's hard to find. I do the same with the largest ship, the carrier. The others I scatter over the grid.

I decide to be magnanimous. "You want to go first?"

"Okay," he says. "D-two."

"Miss."

I see him reach for a white peg to mark that on his vertical target grid.

I wonder if he likes to hide his ships around the edges, too, so I say, "A-ten."

"Miss," he answers. "My turn. C-six."

"Hit." It's my cruiser.

"Ha." He reaches for another peg.

"G-four," I say.

"Miss." He waits for me to put a peg in that spot. Then he calls out, "C-seven."

"Hit," I say, and he grins. I follow with C-three.

"Miss."

We play back and forth, and in a short time he sinks my cruiser, submarine, carrier, and battleship. I've only sunk his carrier—the biggest and easiest to sink. I haven't even hit any others; that's never happened before.

He finally finds my destroyer in the bottom right corner and sinks it, too.

"I win!" he says and laughs. "You can run, but you can't hide."

"So let's see where *you* were hiding," I tell him and turn around his plastic kit. "*What!*"

His ocean grid is empty, except for the carrier that I destroyed. No wonder I couldn't find them; they weren't there.

"Nice," I say and throw his kit back at his laughing face

as Mrs. Taylor stops in the doorway.

Her eyebrows go up, so I say, "Aw, he cheated." It comes out sounding whiny, so I follow it up with an explanation. "He had only one ship set up, so that's the only one I could hit."

Mrs. Taylor ignores that and says, "Boys, Mrs. Clive in room 203 is calling for an LCD projector and screen. Would you please go to the media center, pick them up from Ms. Hadley, and deliver them to Mrs. Clive? Ms. Hadley lost her assistant, and Ms. Derby is working outdoors today."

"The library assistant is lost?" Boot asks.

Mrs. Taylor frowns and looks suspicious, as if she thinks Boot is playing with her. "She lost her job because of budget cuts."

"Idiot." I murmur it but loud enough for him to hear.

His face turns red like Yosemite Sam's, and he looks really mad.

We get up and walk past Mrs. Taylor. In the hall, I lope alongside him. "Battleship requires more luck than skill. In fact, you can be as dumb as *you* are and still win. So why'd you cheat?"

He doesn't look at me but says in a matter-of-fact voice, "Because I hate you."

"But I'm so likable," I say. "I've heard that from . . . oh, at *least* three people. And one of them isn't even related to me."

He ignores me, so I don't say anything more. It's not nearly as much fun being sarcastic with him if he doesn't react.

We get to the media center and find Ms. Hadley sitting at the circulation desk, staring at her computer.

Ms. Hadley knows me pretty well because I'm always down here checking out books. Once in her office I saw a box with an address label that said MARION HADLEY, MEDIA SPECIALIST. So she's Marion the Librarian. I thought that was pretty funny, so I mentioned it to her.

"I know," she said and rolled her eyes. "I started counting how many times people pointed that out to me when I was in library school. I gave up somewhere around eighty-five. That was just the first week."

And I thought I was so clever.

But sometimes I call her Marion the Librarian just to see her smile.

She looks up. "Hi, guys," she says. "Did Mrs. Taylor send you?" I say yes. "I've got what you want." She walks into her office, rolls out the LCD projector on a cart, and nods back over her shoulder. "Mick, the screen's back here in my office. Will you get it for me?"

"Sure."

I go and bring it back. She rolls the cart to Boot. "There you go, Boot," she says. "That's your name, right?"

"Yeah," he tells her.

"Boot and I don't get along," I say, "so Mr. Maddox is having us play games together every day till we call a truce."

"I heard about that," she says. "How's it going?"

It's cool that our fame has spread even to the librarian. I shrug. "Aside from Boot cheating, or pouring peaches in my shoe, or insulting my family, I'd say it's going extremely well."

Marion the Librarian laughs, and Boot looks away.

"And you're giving this your best effort, Mick?" she asks.

"I can honestly tell you that the game room has changed my life for the better," I say.

She laughs, not knowing that I'm perfectly serious. If it hadn't been for the game room, I wouldn't be enjoying my current fame and popularity, and more important, I'd never have kissed Tabitha Slater. Even if I never get to kiss her again, it was the highlight of my life up to this point, and I have the game room to thank for it. That and being able to relentlessly torment Boot Quinn. That started the whole ball rolling.

Boot and I walk out of the media center. I lead the way, carrying the screen, and he's right behind me wheeling the cart.

I'm wishing the bell would ring, so everyone would flow into the hall and see Boot and me running this errand. We could get a lot of mileage out of it. Or more to the point, *I* could get a lot of mileage out of it.

The cart rams into my heel. "Oh, sorry," Boot says. I glance back at him, but I don't say anything.

Jerrod Kitchen comes out of a classroom and sees us. He grins. "Hey, Quinn!"

The cart bashes into my heel again, and this time it hurts.

"Oh, sorry," Boot says. I look back at him. He's trying not to laugh, and he steals a look at Jerrod, who grins back at him.

"You do that one more time—" I say, and he shoves the cart into me one more time. It rams into my leg, and I stagger forward.

I get my balance, reach around the cart, grab the front of Boot's shirt, and yank him up to my face. I'm wondering if his feet are still on the floor.

"I said—" and I'm talking through clenched teeth, "don't *do* that."

He pushes me away but doesn't say anything, and I let go. He walks ahead of me toward room 203, away from Jerrod, who stopped laughing when I hauled Boot off his feet.

I follow him. "Just in case it interests you," I say loud enough for him to hear, "Tabitha called me yesterday afternoon. She asked me to meet her under the Twelfth Avenue

Bridge, and we made out. She's a great kisser, Boot. Whatdaya think of *that*?"

His back stiffens, and I smile.

Gotcha.

CHAPTER THIRTEEN

Boot's Turn

AFTER MICK TOLD ME about kissing Tabitha, the rest of the day turned bad. It had started out great because Jesse and his dad heard from the cops about how I'd caught the perp, and they called to congratulate me before I left for school. Jesse even said he'd give me some guitar lessons for free. And my dad didn't wake me up with water in the face today because he was happy about his promotion and impressed at how I handled myself in the alley last night. And then Tabitha and Cheyanne seemed real impressed with what I did, too.

But when we got back to the game room after Mick told me about the kiss, he beat me five times playing Battleship, all the time smiling that smile that says *I'm better than you at everything*. Then in fifth period, my language arts teacher yelled at me in front of everybody because I didn't read some story we were supposed to read. Like I care about some stupid story.

And all I can think about for most of the day is Mick and Tabitha kissing under the Twelfth Avenue Bridge, and it kind of wipes out all the good stuff that went before it last night and this morning. I shouldn't be surprised; it's always like this. Just when something good happens, something bad comes along and ruins everything. It's the one thing I can always count on.

When the bell rings at the end of the day, I go outside and see J.K. and Clay. We're walking away from the school when I hear somebody call out my name. I turn around and see Tabitha.

She walks over kind of swinging her hips and smiling this big smile. I can't believe it.

"Hey, it's Boot the hero," she says. "Are you going to catch another criminal tonight?"

"I don't know," I say. That sounds really dumb, so I add, "Maybe."

I already told J.K. and Clay about the robbery, so they know what she's talking about.

"If you catch any more bad guys, maybe they'll make a movie about you," she says.

Suddenly I'm thinking maybe I have a chance with her after all. She's looking at me the way she did when I winked at her in the caf. It's like I'm a rock star or something.

"I thought you were meeting Sullivan at his locker," I say, then wish I didn't. Why should I bring *him* up?

"Oh—that's *right*." She smacks her hand on the side of her head. "I guess I forgot."

She *forgot*? Kissing him yesterday and forgetting him today? I'm laughing and whooping it up like crazy in my head, but I play it cool. I look at J.K., and he kind of smiles at me.

She does a quick shrug and goes, "Well, I didn't see him when I was at my locker just now. Maybe he already left."

I smile at her. "Yeah, maybe he did."

"He could've gone to the library," she says. "He says he likes to read a lot, and it's like his second home."

I scrunch up my nose. "He's such a nerd."

She laughs. "It's really funny how you guys hate each other. I wondered why you fight him—he's a *lot* bigger than you. But I realized this morning when you told me about catching that robber—you're just really brave."

I think about that and decide she's right. I don't know anybody else who's tackled a perp during a robbery. "Yeah, I guess I am."

A voice calls out, "Hey, Tabitha."

I look over and see Sullivan walking toward us with Adam and Connor. I can feel my insides jump a little. He gives her this careful smile.

"Thought you were going to meet me at your locker."

"Yeah, sorry, Mick, I forgot. I keep thinking about what Boot did last night. I've never known a hero."

Sullivan looks at me. "Yeah, right, a hero who cheats at Battleship."

Tabitha laughs and gives me a little push. "You do? You cheated in the game room?"

I don't mind the push because she's still looking like I'm a hero, and besides, she can touch me anytime she wants to. I laugh and say, "Yeah, but I only cheat with people I hate. But that's a whole nother story."

"A *whole nother*?" Mick says. "What kind of a word is 'nother'?" He laughs.

"Shut up," I tell him.

Just then Cheyanne and Abby appear. They see we're in an argument, and they laugh.

"I bet you've never darkened a library doorway in your life, have you?" Mick asks. I don't answer, and he says louder, "Have you, Boot?"

"Well," I say, "I hear the library's your second home." He looks quick at Tabitha, and I keep going. "You probably *need* a second home when your dad's drunk, right? I bet he makes lots of noise," and now I pretend I'm drunk and slur my words, "trippin' over the furniture and fallin' down."

Tabitha's eyes get big. "Whoa."

Cheyanne lets out a small laugh.

Mick comes at me, but Adam and Connor grab him. It's all they can do to hold him back.

I just laugh, and that makes Mick madder.

"Be cool, Mick," Connor says.

Mick points at me. "I'll pull your tongue out and wrap it around your neck."

"We're still on school property," Connor says. "Mr. Maddox'll throw you out for good if you get into another fight."

Mick stops pushing at Adam and Connor and stares hard at me. "Okay," he says. "We'll walk down a block, so we're off school property."

"No, come on, Mick," Adam says. "No fighting."

I look around and see that other people are stopping to watch. And I get an idea.

"Okay, then," I say. "'Dare.'"

Mick stares at me. Everybody around here knows the "dare" game.

"I'd get more satisfaction from beating you up," he says. "But I'll settle for humiliation. We'll exchange dares instead of fighting."

"Who goes first?" somebody asks.

"We'll flip a coin," Sullivan says.

He pushes his hand into his jeans pocket and comes out with a quarter. "You call it, Yosemite."

I go, "Heads."

He flips the coin in the air. It makes this arc, falls down, and clinks on the sidewalk, rolls a foot or so, and plunks on its side.

We all go over to look at it. "Heads," I say. J.K. and Clay go, "Yeah!" behind me. I get to call the first dare.

"I can't wait to see what brilliant idea you come up with," Sullivan says. "What's it going to be, Einstein?"

"The rule says you get ten minutes to name it," J.K. tells me.

I can't remember who made up that rule, but pretty much everybody follows it.

"Anybody have a watch?"

Tabitha steps up. "I do." She looks at her watch. "I'll tell you when the time's up."

I turn away from Mick, and J.K. and Clay lean in.

"What are you going to tell him to do?" J.K. asks.

"Maybe I should make him jump off a building," I say.

Clay laughs, but he says, "The rule says it can't be something that would end his life."

"That's right," J.K. says. "No killing or maiming."

"Too bad," I say.

"Yeah," J.K. says. "What's *maiming*, anyway?"

I'm not sure, so I say, "We have to concentrate. We need something good." I see Tabitha trying to hear what we're saying. I get an idea and motion for her to come closer.

"He likes the library, right?"

"Yeah," she says. Her eyes are still really big. "What are you going to dare him to do?"

I haven't been to the library since a field trip in fifth grade, and I can't remember much about what it looks like. But I got a great idea for Mick's dare.

I look over at Mick and see that now there's a bigger crowd of people standing around. They're whispering and watching me.

"We're going to the library," I say, and Mick's face tells me I made the right pick.

"Let's go," I say.

The library is only a couple of blocks away, so the whole crowd heads in that direction. We get there just before the time is up.

When we're in the parking lot, close to the front door, Mick turns to me. "What's the dare?" he asks. He has a scared look on his face, and I'm feeling pretty good about that.

I walk past this statue of an old lady reading to a kid sitting beside her. I point to the side of the building. "Throw paint all over the library, the front door, and all the walls."

Tabitha makes a breathy sound. But she looks kind of excited, too, and so do a bunch of the others. J.K. hoots.

Mick's face turns a whitish color, and he looks like he's going to be sick. *Cool.*

"You want me to throw paint on it—now?"

"No, stupid," I tell him. "We'll come back when it's dark, around ten o'clock tonight. I'll bring the paint."

He doesn't say anything for a while. He just stands there and stares at the library door like he's thinking about it. He looks over at Tabitha, then at the ground, then back at Tabitha again.

"I'll be there," he says in a real serious voice.

I can hear everybody talking. Some are saying they're coming back tonight. They're all pretty excited.

So am I. I can't wait to watch Mick throw paint all over his second home.

CHAPTER FOURTEEN

Mick's Turn

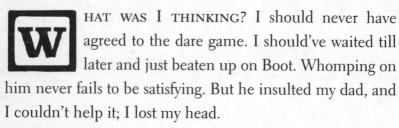HAT WAS I THINKING? I should never have agreed to the dare game. I should've waited till later and just beaten up on Boot. Whomping on him never fails to be satisfying. But he insulted my dad, and I couldn't help it; I lost my head.

I get home and sit in my room and stare out the window. *I'm going to vandalize the library? Why would I do something so disgusting that I feel sick when I think about it? Because of my new fame? Am I afraid of losing the first chance I've ever had to be in the limelight? Or is it because of Tabitha?* Whatever the answers are to these questions, they'll probably point out the rather obvious fact that I'm a superficial jerk.

Boot knew I called the library my "second home," and it's clear who told him. Only three people know that, and two of them don't even know Boot. It had to be Tabitha.

So now I'm wondering *how* she told him. Did they laugh about it? Or did she just mention it in passing?

I think about pouring paint all over the library, Nana's and my special place. It'll be like splashing paint on her grave. And all over my own room.

I shake my head, even though nobody's here to see it. *I'm such an idiot.*

Okay, that's it. I can't do it. I *won't.*

I nod, even though there's still no one here to see it. I can't believe I was such a sheep, going along with the expectation of the crowd.

Amazing. I feel better instantly. Maybe I'm not a superficial jerk after all.

The phone rings, and I pick up the receiver on my bedside table.

"Mick?" It's Tabitha.

"Hey," I say. And in spite of everything, all those jets in my chest roar into the sky for a spectacle of soaring and swooping.

"So you're going to dump the paint on the library building? You guys are amazing."

"What do you mean?" I ask her.

"Neither of you ever backs down," she says. "You're both so strong, and you don't take any crap from each other."

"Well . . ."

"I know you like the library, and that you're there all the

time 'cause you like to read."

"You told Boot?" I ask her.

"Yeah. I just happened to mention it. Are you mad at me?"

She actually sounds concerned that I might be mad. I wasn't exactly mad at first. Maybe disappointed and suspicious. But I'm pretty sure she likes me. She probably just said it when she was talking to Boot about me. How could I stay mad at Tabitha Slater, especially when she's talking about *me*?

"No," I say. "I'm not mad."

"Good." She sounds relieved. "Well, I'll be at the library tonight at ten. And afterward, maybe we can take a walk?"

Tabitha Slater is asking me to walk with her again. Oh, man. A walk in the dark could easily lead to other, even more pleasant things. So now I'm heavily conflicted: in my mind, a despicable act is in a violent battle with the very best thing I can think of.

Then an idea occurs to me. Maybe I could volunteer—since I'm a library regular—to clean the paint off the building. Tomorrow is Friday, so I could do it after school. I'd be able to do both, and my conscience—which doesn't get much exercise, I have to admit—would be satisfied.

That's it. A middle ground, sort of.

"Mick?"

She startles me from my thoughts. "Oh. Sure. Afterward, we can take a walk."

"Great! See you then."

We hang up, and I pace around the room again, the second time in two minutes. I keep thinking about it: I'm about to deface a building I love. I'll be a vandal, a superficial jerk, a sleazeball with no integrity.

And all because of a girl.

Mom and I have supper without Dad. I've been thinking so much about breaking the law that I forgot he was going to meet his brother for dinner at Jamboree. But when I see Mom set only two places at the table, I remember.

"What time is Dad meeting Dave?" I ask her after we sit down to eat. I find it hard to call the man "Uncle Dave." I don't even know the guy.

"Six," Mom says, glancing into the kitchen at the clock on the wall, which reads six fifteen.

Maybe Dave will be a good influence on Dad because he doesn't drink anymore. And it'll be easier for Dad to abstain if his brother is drinking something harmless, like soda.

But Mom looks anxious.

"It'll be okay," I tell her.

She reaches over and squeezes my hand.

I can't look at her because it's hard to see all that worry and hope in her eyes. She's spent a lot of years looking like that.

So I trace a line of wood grain in the table with my finger and say again, "It'll be okay."

I just hope I know what I'm talking about.

It's nearly ten o'clock when I slip out of the house. Dad hasn't come home yet, and I know that's a bad sign. I told Mom I was going to bed. She's staring at the TV in her bedroom—probably not even hearing the local news—so I feel more guilty than ever sneaking out. But I don't have time to think about it.

I have some vandalism to do.

What a horrible thought. The planes in my chest are not only *not* soaring, they've all crash-landed into my stomach, and now they lie there on fire, in a heap of twisted metal and flames.

When I arrive at the library, a small crowd is waiting for me. Great. Lots of witnesses to my degradation.

The library closed at eight o'clock, so the place is dark. The parking lot is lit up, though, by bright vapor lights overhead. One of the lights stands directly over the statue, shining down on the grandmother and boy. Nana and me.

First I see J. K. and Matt Thumm standing together. Then I see Adam and Connor.

Tabitha and Cheyanne are at the edge of the crowd. Tabitha's chewing on a strand of hair, so I guess she's nervous, too. She waves at me but doesn't move.

Boot elbows his way out of the crowd, holding a can of paint.

Now I start to sweat. I look around for cops cruising in the street. They might stop to check out a bunch of loitering teenagers, even if they happen to be standing in front of the public library. But I don't see any. Or anyone else, other than the people from my school.

Everybody murmurs and watches me approach.

Boot stops in front of me and sets the can of paint on the cement with a heavy *thunk*. He straightens up. He's got a cigarette between his fingers, and the smoke trails up into the night sky. I stare at the can of paint.

"That's a full can?" I ask him.

"Almost." He smiles. "It's red."

"Wonderful," I say.

He holds up a can opener that he's just taken from his pocket.

"And you even came prepared," I say. "Very Boy Scout of you."

Boot squats next to the paint can and opens it.

"Okay," he says, standing up again. "Do it. All over the front door and the walls."

He stops and seems to notice the statue for the first time.

"And this, too. Start with this."

Nana's and my statue.

I glance over at Tabitha. She comes over and puts a hand on my arm.

"Just get it over with," she says.

Adam counsels me from the edge of the crowd. "Make sure no one's around, Mick."

"You mean, other than these eighty-seven people?" I say and point to the crowd he's standing in.

Tabitha gives my arm a gentle squeeze.

I pick up the paint can and walk to the statue. I can't look at it while I'm defacing it, and I can't let myself think about it, so I turn my head and dump a lot of red paint over the top of the grandmother's head.

A murmur comes from the crowd. I hear Boot laugh.

I have to look now—the paint slides over the woman's head and face, and down onto the boy's head and shoulders, and all over the book they're reading. It pools on the cement around their feet. The paint left on the statue puddles in small crevices in the grandmother's and boy's hair and ears and shoulders, and on the book, and on their laps. The red paint on the dark metal looks like blood under the vapor lights. I feel as if I've killed the two friends who I've known since I was a little kid.

A wave of nausea hits me.

"Now the front door," Boot says. He's squinting through the smoke from the cigarette in his mouth, but he's got a smile on his face.

I have a sudden urge to dump the rest of the paint on top of his head. But I don't.

If I did, I wouldn't get my turn to dare him. And after this, I'm going to think up a dare that's devastating.

I walk up to the door and stop.

I hear snickers behind me.

"Do it," Boot says.

I pour paint on the front door and then throw the rest on the brick wall.

The paint runs fast down the glass door and onto the cement. It also splashes a dark red stain that collects in the crevices of the brick and runs down the wall onto the grass. I drop the paint can.

Someone calls out, "There's a cop!" and everybody takes off in different directions as a cruiser slows in front of the library.

I run behind the library and down an alley. On the other side of a garage nearby, my stomach finally lurches, and I throw up onto the grass.

When I'm finished, I wipe my mouth with my hand and I remember I promised Tabitha a walk. I look around, but I don't see anyone.

That's okay. I don't feel like seeing her. I lean against the garage.

Even if I didn't have vomit-breath, I don't feel like kissing her.

I push off of the garage, run a hand over my head, and look around again to make sure the police cruiser isn't turning into the alley.

It's quiet with nobody around.

I trudge to the street, across in the darkest area between streetlights, and head toward home.

CHAPTER FIFTEEN

Boot's Turn

IT WAS COOL WATCHING Mick throw paint all over the statue and the front of the library—especially because he looked mad and scared and sad while he was doing it.

Serves him right for always acting like he's better than me.

I looked at Tabitha a few times, and she seemed pretty excited about it. I know she was watching me, too, to see my reaction, so I laughed.

When the cops drive by and everybody runs, I cut through the alley behind the Dairy Queen and end up walking down Shannon Street. I see Tabitha up ahead with Cheyanne. They're going into the HandiMart.

I go in, too, and walk along the candy aisle, pretending I don't see them. She spots me in about five seconds, and they both run over.

"Did the police catch anybody?" Tabitha asks. Her eyes are big, and her cheeks are red.

"I dunno," I say. "I don't think so."

"I was scared we'd get caught," Tabitha says.

"Me, too," Cheyanne chimes in. "I didn't see any of the cops get out of their cars or chase anybody."

Tabitha laughs. "Maybe they've been eating too many doughnuts."

"Prob'ly," I say.

"It's a good thing the cops didn't have anyone like *you* on their side," Tabitha says. "They'd have caught Mick for sure. You would've tackled him."

I shrug like it's not a big thing that she gave me a compliment. "Yeah, I guess."

"I wonder if you'll get a hero award or something," she says. "I mean, for catching the thief yesterday." She laughs. "Not for daring Mick to dump paint on the library."

"Well," I say, "did I tell you that the owners of River City Music called me to thank me for saving their store?"

"Yeah," Tabitha says. "I think so." She looks at Cheyanne who nods.

"That's all the reward I need," I say. I hope she notices that I'm pretty modest. "Jesse, the son of the owner—he plays in a great band—he's my best friend, so I knew how expensive those guitars are. I wouldn't want Jesse and his family to go bankrupt or anything."

"Mick sure hated having to dump that paint," she says.

And Cheyanne goes, "Did you see his face?"

"He was miserable," Tabitha says. She's smiling. "You guys are nuts! I wonder what he'll do to you next time when it's *his* turn?"

That stops me. I haven't had time to think about that. We're exchanging dares, so pretty soon, Mick will give me one. And I'll have to do it, or I'll look like a wuss.

But I don't want to think about that now.

For a second, I wonder about Tabitha saying that me and Mick are nuts. I think she meant it as a compliment, but I'm not totally sure. She looks like she's having fun, so I figure at least it wasn't a huge insult.

"Well, see ya," she says. "Keep us posted."

"Hunh?" I say.

"On your fights with Mick."

"Oh, sure."

She waves and leaves with Cheyanne, and I turn away, my face heating up.

Geez, I'm so dense sometimes.

When I get home, Dad doesn't ask where I've been. He just looks up from the couch where he's watching the 10:00 news on TV and says, "You finally decide to come home?"

"Yeah," I say. I kind of laugh to see if he's kidding.

He turns back to the TV and rolls a toothpick in his

mouth from one side to the other. "You coulda told me you'd be out late."

"I didn't think you'd mind," I tell him. He usually doesn't say anything when I come home late.

"You better not oversleep again," he says, still focusing on the TV.

I sit on the big chair. "I won't."

He doesn't talk for minute, and I stare at a stain on the carpet and try to think of something to say that might put him in a better mood. "Did you think any more about what kind of car you're going to buy?"

He's not listening. He puts up a hand. "I want to see this."

A story is on the news about an armed robbery at a convenience store across town. He sits forward and stares hard at the screen. "Anybody get killed?" He asks it loudly as if the announcer can hear him.

"I think we missed that part," I say.

"That's 'cause you were talking," he says.

By the time the story is over, we find out that no one was hurt, but the robbers got away with an undisclosed amount of money from the cash register.

"Those cops don't know what they're doing," he mutters. "They're a bunch of idiots."

"The guys who were called after the River City Music break-in were okay," I say.

"They're *all* idiots. You shouldn't have had to do their work for them."

I wonder what he'd say if I'd been picked up for vandalism tonight. I don't know, and I don't want to find out.

Ethan was arrested a couple of years ago at a rock concert for getting in a fight. Dad bailed him out of jail, but when they got home, he and Ethan yelled at each other and got in a shoving match before Ethan ran off for two days. I still don't know where he went. But when he came back, they'd both calmed down, and neither one of them talked about it again, as far as I know.

I head through the kitchen to go down to my room, but the phone rings.

Dad calls out, "Get that, will you?"

I grab the receiver.

"Hey, Boot."

I swallow. I'm pretty sure it's Tabitha.

"Hey," I say.

"Who is it?" Dad yells.

"Um, just a minute," I say and put the phone down. I go into the living room. "It's for me," I tell him quietly. "I'm going to take it in my room."

"Okay," he says without looking up from the TV.

I run downstairs, sit on the edge of my bed, and pick up the phone.

"Hello?"

"Hi, Boot. It's Tabitha."

I'm pretty nervous about her calling me, but I try to act relaxed. "Hey, Tab. What's up?" I say.

"I was just thinking," she says. The TV upstairs is pretty loud, so I have trouble hearing her, even though I'm listening with my good ear. "Mick was so mad about the dare. I bet he'll think of some really horrible dare for you."

That stops me like it did at the HandiMart. I don't want to think about it, but I figure maybe I'd better.

"I'll handle it," I tell her.

My dad drops the receiver on the phone, and it clatters and then cuts off. Good. I'll hear better now.

"Do you want me to try to find out what he's going to make you do?" she asks.

That surprises me, and I'm like, "You think you can?"

"Maybe," she says. "I can try. I know him pretty well."

She doesn't have to tell me. "Okay," I say, and I'm thinking about them kissing under the Twelfth Avenue Bridge.

"I'll talk to him tomorrow," she says.

I wonder why she's offering to do this. *Isn't she his girlfriend?*

So I ask her. "Aren't you sort of going out with him?"

I can hear the smile in her voice when she says, "Yeah, sort of." She laughs. "You guys are both nuts, though. But you're both really brave and—well, it's funny that you guys hate each other so much."

"Funny?" I ask.

"Yeah," she says. "It's like this big contest. Like who's going to start the fight *this* time? And who will win? And what'll happen next?"

"Oh. Yeah." I don't know what else to say.

"How come you guys fight all the time? I mean, why do you guys hate each other so much? I'm just curious."

"I don't know," I say. No one had ever asked me that before. "I just hate him. He's ugly and stupid, and he thinks he's so smart."

She laughs. "Okay, if you say so. Hey, I'll see you tomorrow. And I'll try to find out what dare he's going to give you."

"Okay," I say.

"See ya."

"See ya."

I hang up and stare at the wall. That was one weird conversation. I mean, she seems to like me. And she wants to help me by finding out what dare Mick will give me. But a bigger question fills my mind, and I have no idea what the answer is.

Who's side is she on, anyway?

CHAPTER SIXTEEN

Mick's Turn

I UNLOCK THE FRONT door and step inside. Light from a fluorescent fixture under a kitchen cupboard spills into the living room. It wasn't on when I left, so that means that Dad got home, or Mom turned it on for him.

I close the door quietly behind me.

"Herb?" Mom's voice comes from the hall. She shuffles into view and stops, surprised. She holds her old pink robe closed at the waist. "Mick?" She runs a hand through her messy hair, squinting in the light from the kitchen. "I thought you were in bed."

"Oh. I—I went for a walk."

She's thinking about Dad, so it doesn't register. She sinks onto the couch.

"He didn't get home yet?" I ask.

"No." She stares across the room, and a long moment passes. "Mick," she finally says, "I don't know if I can do this anymore."

I'm afraid I know what she's saying. I feel my body stiffen, so I purposely try to relax my muscles. I wait for her to go on.

"It's been too many years of broken promises," she says. "He says he'll stop drinking, and he does for a while, but . . ." Her voice drifts off for a moment. "I don't want to live the rest of my life this way."

I sit down next to her.

"Does Dad know how you feel?"

Her hand waves in a dismissive gesture. "Oh, I've been warning him for the entire fourteen years we've been married."

My mind stops on that. *I'm* fourteen. I thought they got married a year before I was born.

Is she not counting accurately, or did she get pregnant and have to marry him? Was I a *little accident*?

"My warnings don't mean anything to him because that's all they've been—" she says. "Just empty threats."

My mind is still on the fourteen years part, so it takes a second or two to play back in my mind what she said.

"Are you going to take a stand this time?" I ask.

I'm almost as jumpy as when I'm with Tabitha. I don't want them to split up, but I don't know if Dad will ever stop drinking. He's always falling off the wagon.

Or stepping off. Or leaping.

"I don't know, honey," she says. "I'm thinking about it. One thing I'm not doing anymore for sure is call his work and say he's sick when he's off drinking somewhere or sleeping it off."

For the last year or so I've been looking forward to the day when I'm eighteen and can get out on my own. One thing I want to get away from is Dad's drinking.

Why wouldn't Mom feel the same way?

My head is crowded with questions about what would happen to Mom and me if she leaves him. *Would we move out? Where would we live?* She doesn't make much money at her job.

And Dad. I don't know if he can survive without her.

Maybe I'd need to stay with him, so he'll get up and go to work. And eat. And have clean clothes. And—this is depressing.

"Why is this time different?" I ask her.

She sighs. "It's not. It's just the first time I've talked to you about it." She looks at me and blinks. "Are you okay?"

"Sure," I lie. *I just committed vandalism to impress a girl, my dad's probably passed out somewhere, and my mom's thinking about moving out.* "I'm fine."

"Why don't you go to bed," she says.

I don't think I can sleep. "Okay."

I start to get up.

"Mick?" She stops me with her hand on my arm. "We'd be okay," she says. "I mean, if your dad and I split up. You and I'd get an apartment somewhere nearby."

But what about Dad? "Okay."

She reads my mind. "It might be the best thing for your dad. He hasn't hit bottom in all these years, but losing his family would 'raise the bottom,' like they say in AA."

How does she know what they say in AA?

"Maybe it would wake him up, and he'd stop drinking for good," she says.

"And maybe he and Dave are just drinking Cokes and going over old times," I say, straightening up. I don't believe it for a minute.

She doesn't, either, because she lets it go without comment. "Let's both go to bed." She gets up but stops and frowns at me. "You went out for a walk? This late?"

Oops.

"I wasn't sleepy," I say.

She nods. "We're both worried about him." She puts her arms around me. "We'll be okay, honey." (I can't help but notice she's gone from 'we *would* be okay' to 'we *will* be okay' just in a few seconds. She's making plans.) "I have most of the inheritance money from Grandpa."

I hug her back, wondering if the money is enough to cover the difference between her meager earnings at Josephine's and what we need to live on. But I don't ask.

"Night," I say.

"Night, honey."

Dad hasn't come home by the time I wake up the next morning. I know because I find Mom sitting bleary-eyed, curled over the dining room table, stirring her coffee. She hasn't gotten dressed for work yet.

"Morning," I say.

"Morning, honey." She doesn't look up.

I shake some Cheerios into a bowl, splash on some milk, and sit across the table from her. Seeing her like this causes the familiar ache in my chest to reappear. I wonder if Dad knows what his drinking does to her. Probably not. Or maybe he doesn't care. Or maybe his need to drink blots it out.

She doesn't talk to me, and I don't feel much like talking, either. The only sound is the clanking of my spoon against the bowl and the crunching I hear inside my head as I chew.

After school I'm going to stop by the library and scrub the paint off the statue and the building. *If it comes off.* The only thing that keeps me from getting totally depressed is the thought that Boot will have to take whatever dare I dish out to him. He's built such a rep at school as a tough guy, he *can't* refuse a reciprocal dare, or he'll lose face with all his buddies.

"I'm stopping at the library on my way home from school," I tell Mom.

"Okay," she says. This time she looks up at me. "Sorry, I'm not very communicative."

"It's okay," I tell her. "I'm not, either. See you tonight."

On my way to school, I realize I'm loping more slowly than usual. The resentment about Dad's drinking has climbed on my back again. I bend forward, shouldering the old, familiar load.

If he just wanted to make himself miserable, that would be one thing. But Mom is another story. She doesn't deserve misery.

I get to school before the bell and wait outside. The news about my vandalism is running wildly through the crowd of people gathered outside. I can tell because they whisper to each other and glance over at me. Some look shocked; some of them laugh a little.

"Hey, Mick." Adam and Connor stroll over. They look serious.

"Tell him," Connor says to Adam, nudging him with his elbow.

Adam rolls his eyes.

"What?" I say. "Tell me what?"

"Adam doesn't want to tell you," Connor says, "but I think you should know."

"Spill it," I tell Adam, and I don't care that I sound

crabby. "I'm not in a mood for games today."

"You know Tabitha Slater?" Adam says. "We've seen you with her enough, so we know you like her."

"Yeah, so?" I say. The adrenaline starts to pump through my body.

"Well," he says, "Cheyanne told Jason Parsons that Tabitha's taking bets on your fights with Boot."

"What do you mean?" I ask.

"Well, when you guys fight—" Adam says, "she takes bets on which one of you will win the next round. The people who guess right divide the money after she takes her ten percent. She keeps score with slash marks on the wall in the girls' locker room."

"So she makes money no matter who wins?" I ask.

"Right," Connor says. "All the girls check the wall every day they have P.E. And sometimes when they don't."

I let that sink in.

"And," Adam adds, "she's making some pretty good cash because of you guys."

"So whatever Tabitha says to you," Connor tells me, "keep that in mind. She's a bookie. She *wants* you and Boot to fight. You're tied right now. So everybody's waiting for the next one."

The importance of this news sweeps over me. *She's using me to make money?*

"I thought you'd want to know," Connor says.

Do I want to know? I'm not sure.

"Yeah," I say. "Thanks."

"See you," Adam says. He and Connor walk off.

I stare into the trees, trying to decide what this all means.

Does Tabitha genuinely like me, and she started doing this for fun as an afterthought? Or has she been using me from the beginning to make money on our fights?

And most of all: *Did this start before or after the kiss?*

She acts like she likes me best, but she always wants to talk about Boot and our fights. *Is jealousy one of her tactics?*

The bell rings, and I go inside with everyone else.

I'm standing at my locker when Tabitha materializes at my side. I'm not sure whether I'm happy to see her or not.

"Hey, Mick," Tabitha says. She's smiling. "The cops didn't catch you last night, did they?"

"No," I answer.

"I was so scared!" she tells me. "Cheyanne and I saw Boot at the HandiMart afterward, so we know he got away."

I find myself watching her differently. Before this morning, I hoped to see any signal that she was interested in me. Now I'm examining her face and listening to every word to see if I can find any hint of manipulation.

But I'm not sure what that looks like on Tabitha. The only person I've been aware of trying to manipulate me is my dad trying to turn me into an athlete. He's about as subtle as a bulldozer. I don't know if Tabitha has a playbook of strategies for this scheme of hers and how obvious she is when she uses them.

"Was it awful pouring the paint on the statue?" she asks. Her face is eager, waiting to hear my answer.

"It's not my favorite leisure activity," I say.

She laughs.

I don't want to believe Adam, and, in a way, I wish he hadn't told me. *Who knows? Maybe it isn't even true. Maybe Cheyanne made it up. But why would she do that?*

"What are you going to dare Boot to do?" she asks.

I search her face, but I don't see signs of guile. And she *looks* as if she likes me. If she's acting, she deserves an Oscar for her performance. *Best Actress in an Eighth-Grade Scheme.*

"I haven't decided," I say. "You have any suggestions?"

That's when I remember how she told Boot that the library was my second home. *Did she help him think of a dare?*

She laughs again. "No." She reaches out and touches my arm. "Want me to think about it?"

I shrug. "Sure."

"Hey," she says, her voice a little lower, "we didn't take our walk last night."

"I know."

"How about after school?" Her face looks innocent and hopeful. And there's that hand on my arm.

Those airplanes must have been patched up with miraculous speed because they're tearing down the runways and roaring into the air again.

"Yeah," I say. "Let's do."

"Great." Her smile is dazzling. "See you."

"Yeah, see you."

She flounces off down the hall.

I watch her go. To say that I'm conflicted is an understatement. I'm suspicious and scared and happy.

Stunt planes, along with the regular jets, are hotdogging in the air, narrowly missing the others who take evasive action to avoid midair collisions.

Tabitha, now at the end of the hall, waves at somebody and hurries out of sight.

Is she rushing to tell one of her friends the latest news about my dumping paint on the library? Or maybe she's just arguing that the dares definitely qualify as fights. If they buy her argument, she wins. The more slashes on the wall, the more money she makes.

On the other hand, she might be hurrying to tell Cheyanne that we're going for another walk—and she's planning on making out again. *Does she daydream about kissing the way I do?*

I shake my head and marvel. That girl is full of surprises. I'm just wondering if I'll end up liking her. Or not.

CHAPTER SEVENTEEN

Boot's Turn

EVERYBODY'S TALKING ABOUT the dare I gave Mick last night. It's about the only topic of conversation this morning. The Water Street kids thump me on the back and act as if I'm a hero. In fact, they seem more impressed with that than when I captured the robber at River City Music. I guess it's because of Mick. He might live near Water Street, but he acts like he grew up on the south side, so nobody from my neighborhood likes him.

I don't see him till game-room time. He's sitting on the old couch in the main office. He doesn't look at me when I sit on a chair about four seats down from him. The principal comes out of his inner office.

"Come on back," he says.

We get up and follow him into the game room.

He gestures to the couch, so we sit there. We're as far

away from each other as we can get without sitting on the arms or falling on the floor.

"Okay," he says, taking a seat on the other side of the coffee table. "We're at the end of the week. How's it going?"

We don't say anything at first. Mick shifts in his chair and clears his throat. "I don't think playing games is going to help."

The principal frowns. "What do you mean?"

"I mean," he says, "Boot and I've been . . . let's say *non-friends* since we first met. It's hard to acclimate to different rules in just three days when we're so used to our old patterns."

Jerk. What a show-off.

He turns to me. "Boot, what do you have to say?"

Even though I'm not sure what Mick said exactly, I answer, "I think . . . what he said."

Mick rolls his eyes.

"Okay." He nods and looks at the floor. When he looks up, he goes, "I don't really know you two very well. Mick, what's your favorite way to spend your time?"

Mick glares at me, then says, "I like to read."

His eyebrows go up. "Great. Like what?"

"Lots of different kinds of fiction. I guess I read more thrillers than anything else. You know, Koontz and King. And I like Jeffery Deaver."

"I read those guys, too," he says. "You ever read Marcia Muller?"

"No."

"Check her out. I think you'd like her suspense novels."

Mick seems surprised. "Okay. I will."

He turns to me. "Boot? What about you?"

I look out the window and try to think of something that sounds okay. "Well, I like to play my guitar and stuff."

"Really?" He kind of perks up again. "What's your favorite kind of music to play?"

"Rock. I really like Springsteen. I want to be in a band like his."

He smiles. "Springsteen, huh? He's been one of my favorites for a long time." I try to imagine the principal kicking back in his office, listening to Springsteen, but it's too weird, and the picture doesn't form in my mind. "Do you take guitar lessons?"

"I've had a few. I'm going to get more lessons for free 'cause I caught a robber at River City Music."

"You what? You caught a robber?" He looks real surprised.

I glance at Mick. His jaw looks like it was carved in granite.

I tell the principal about tackling the thief and how Jesse and his dad called me the next day. "Jesse's my best friend," I say.

"Well, it looks like we've got a hero walking our halls," he says and kind of smiles. "Sounds pretty dangerous, too. That took some courage."

I look away and kind of nod. I hope Mick is noticing that the principal is impressed. He probably really hates that.

"Well, it sounds like you deserve those extra guitar lessons," the principal says. "Will you bring your guitar to school sometime soon? I'd like to hear you play."

"Sure."

"Well," he says, "even though you think the games won't help, I want you to continue. I'll check in again with you sometime early next week and see how it's going. What are you playing today?"

I shrug.

"Mick?"

"I don't know. Jenga, I guess."

"Okay with you, Boot?"

"Yeah."

"Have you both played it before?" he asks.

"I've played it," I say.

"I'll let you get started," he says and walks out.

Mick doesn't move. He sits there watching me.

I stare him down.

"You happy how I vandalized the library?" he finally asks. "You like it with red paint all over it?"

"Yeah," I say. "I'm jumping up and down, I'm so happy."

"You better get ready for your turn," he says. "Because I have a dare for you that'll give you nightmares for weeks."

My body freezes. But I don't want him to think I'm

scared, so I will myself to lift my chin and say, "I'm ready."
But I can't stand it, so I say, "What's the dare?"

He gives me this evil smile. "Wouldn't you like to know?"

"Tabitha called me last night." I blurt it out just to make
him feel bad. And it does, I can tell. He tries not to react, but
there's a small change in his eyes, like something moving
underwater.

"So what, Boot?" he says.

I get an idea. "You know the other day when you kissed
her?" I say. "Under the bridge?" He just stares. "Well, she
says it turned her stomach. Made her sick."

The look on Mick's face is perfect. His jaw moves to one
side, and I can see the pain in his eyes.

He doesn't do anything for a few seconds. Then he says,
"That's a great story, Boot. But I don't believe you."

"Yes, you do," I say, and I smile because I can tell he
really *does* believe it. "Yes, you do."

I pick up the Jenga box feeling pretty good. "So. You
wanna play Jenga now?"

He doesn't move, so I open the box and slide out the
Jenga blocks.

We start playing, but I can tell that Mick isn't paying
attention. He acts kind of like a robot. No matter who knocks
down the tower of blocks, he doesn't react. His eyes have a
shiny and faraway look.

We play about ten rounds of Jenga, and for that whole

time, we don't say one word to each other—which is fine with me.

But just before the bell rings ending our time in the game room, he finally comes out of his trance.

"I'll see you after school," he says. "I'm ready to collect on the dare. Meet me at the Corner, and I'll tell you what it is.

The rest of the afternoon, I'm nervous. I tell J.K. that Mick's going to give me the dare, and he tells Clay and Matt. They meet me at my locker, and we walk to the Corner. We go in and buy Cokes, even though I don't want one. I'm too jumpy, but I open mine and drink a little.

We go outside, and I lean against the bike rack. J.K., Clay, and Matt talk about some sports cars in the parking lot, but I don't listen. My head is filled up with wondering about the dare. Maybe I shouldn't have made up that stuff about Tabitha getting sick when Mick kissed her. It made him feel horrible like I wanted, but he's going to find a way to make me pay big time.

In a while, Mick comes walking up the street with Adam and Connor. He doesn't seem to be mad, but he looks real serious. He stops right in front of me.

"It's payback time, Boot," he says.

I hear someone yell, and I look past Mick. Tabitha and some people are running toward us.

"Hey!" she yells. "What's going on? Why didn't you wait for me, Mick?"

Mick doesn't say anything, but he watches her as she slows to a walk about twenty yards away.

Abby and Cheyanne are with Tabitha.

"What's going on?" Tabitha asks.

"I'm giving him the dare," Mick says. He doesn't smile or act like a smart-ass the way he usually does.

Tabitha looks surprised. "Oh."

"Tabitha doesn't want to miss it," Connor tells Mick. Mick nods but doesn't look at Tabitha or Connor. He looks right at me.

"You ready, Boot?" he asks.

"Yeah," I say. "What is it?"

"You know that music store that your best friend owns?" he says.

I stop breathing for a few seconds. I can feel my back go ramrod straight.

"Yeah."

Mick's stare drills into my head. "I want you to go into that store and steal something. And bring it outside."

Something shoots through my body, and it feels like lightning.

The girls go, "What? Steal something?" like they're real surprised.

For the first time, Mick's mouth goes into a little smile.

"And I don't mean a guitar pick or something small," he says. "I want to see you carry out something at least as big as a trumpet. Or a clarinet. Bring it to me. We'll watch from across the street."

Cheyanne lets out a laugh.

"When?" I ask.

"Now, stupid," he says. "Right now."

It's about the worst dare I could get. I've shoplifted a few things before: candy and gum from the Corner; once I stuffed a flashlight under my sweatshirt at the hardware store and walked out with it just to see if I could. Later, I went back and got some batteries so I could turn it on.

But stealing from River City Music would be stealing from my best friend. Jesse and his dad have been really nice. They got enough trouble with their competition across town. And now I have to add to it by ripping them off.

Tabitha is smiling at me, her eyes all alert and excited. J.K. nods to me, like he expects me to go through with it.

Mick looks serious now. "Let's go," he says.

We walk down the street, and I feel numb. I can't believe I'm about to steal from Jesse. It's not right. If he finds out, he'll hate me. I don't even want to think about that.

I hear Tabitha and her friends whispering. I point my

good ear toward her, but I can't hear what they're saying.

Then I think of something that makes me feel a little better. It was pretty cold today, so I've got my jacket on. If I can walk something out of the store under my jacket without anyone seeing, I'll be able to walk it back in a day or two. I'll put it back in an out-of-the-way place and disappear. They'll know something was taken, but when they find it again, they'll think some customer just moved it.

At least I hope so.

It takes us about twenty minutes to get to River City Music. Mick stops across the street, and everybody gathers around him.

"Okay," Mick says. He nods to me. "Do it."

Tabitha smiles. "You can do it, Boot," she says. "Just don't get caught."

Mick looks at her, but he doesn't say anything.

I cross the street and almost get hit by a car that I don't see coming. It blares its horn, and I jump about a foot off the ground. The car swerves away and barrels down the street. My mind is kind of fuzzy, I guess. I didn't even look for traffic.

I have to be sharp now. I have to be aware of everything if I'm going to pull this off.

I stand on the sidewalk and look through the window. I can see Mr. Bramer—Jesse's dad—moving around inside. He stops next to a lady who's looking at a guitar.

I order myself to walk in the door, and my feet do it, putting one in front of the other. I feel the stares of everybody across the street watching my back as I let the heavy door swing shut behind me. I hope no one inside the store sees them. It could look like something fishy is going on.

I check around the store. Jesse isn't here. Maybe he had something going on after school. Maybe he's practicing with his band. Or maybe he's out running an errand. Only Jesse's dad is working today.

I look around. *What can I steal that's small enough to hide under my jacket but big enough that Mick won't say I have to do it again?*

I walk past the counter with the cash register and wander around the store, looking for something the right size. There's a wall of sheet music. Music would be easy to stick under my jacket, but Mick will say it's not big enough, and I'd have to come back. I see an autoharp on a table, but that's too big, so I keep looking. Keyboards are too big, and earplugs are too small. I see some karaoke CDs and some percussion wood blocks. They aren't big enough.

"Hi there, Boot."

I'm so startled, my whole body jerks. I turn to see Jesse's dad. He's smiling at me.

"Hi, Mr. B.," I say, and I sound kind of breathless.

"Didn't mean to startle you," he says.

I shrug and try to look as natural as I can. But when I *am* natural, I'm not thinking about it. So what do I do when I'm acting natural?

"How's everything going for you, son?" he asks.

The *son* stabs a hole through me. "Fine." It comes out a little squeaky.

A man comes in and asks about clarinet reeds. Mr. Bramer nods at me and goes to help him.

I can't do this. I can't steal from Mr. Bramer. He's been nicer to me than even Jesse.

I swing around and look out the front window. Everybody's still there. They look like they're talking and joking around and then glance over here, as if they expect me to come out pretty soon.

I'm jumpier than I've ever been in my whole life. *What should I do?*

If I get caught, Jesse and his dad won't like me anymore. They're the best friends I have.

But if I don't do it, Mick will say I'm a *wuss*, Tabitha will stop paying attention to me, and my friends from Water Street might not want to hang out with me anymore.

If I can just take something without getting caught, I'll have everything. Everyone will like me, and I can return what I stole when no one's looking.

I go back to trying to look natural. I'm usually hanging out by the guitars when I'm in here, so I'm in the right part of the store, anyway. I want to relax, so I don't look stiff and self-conscious.

Then I see the flute. It's not in a case, but just sitting on top of this table on a piece of black velvet or something, and the fluorescent lights on the ceiling shine down, and the silver gleams. It's not as big as a trumpet, but I can't hide anything that big under my jacket.

I look over at where Mr. B. is standing with the man looking for clarinet reeds. He says, "Just a minute," to the man and goes through a door into the back part of the store.

I have to do it now. I can still see everybody across the street waiting for me.

I pick up the flute and stick one end into the waist of my jeans. I hide the rest under my jacket and zip it shut.

And I head for the door. The flute sticks into my leg as I walk, so I'm not walking natural. But I get to the door and open it. The people across the street see me and smile. But then they suddenly look scared and turn away.

I'm out on the sidewalk when a hand claps me on the shoulder from behind. I jerk my head around to see Jesse.

"I can't believe it," he says.

He grabs my jacket and yanks it open. He pulls the flute out. He looks at it wrapped in his fist, then he glares at me, and anger takes over his face.

"A *flute*?" he yells. "You stole a *flute*? That doesn't even make *sense*!"

"I just—I . . ."

I start to tell him it was just a dare, and I was going to bring it back. But I can't make my mouth say it. It's too lame, and he'd never believe it.

I see pain mixed in with all the anger on his face, and I close my mouth.

Mr. Bramer opens the door and says quietly, "Both of you come inside."

I quick look across the street. Mick is the only person left standing there watching.

And he looks real proud of himself.

CHAPTER EIGHTEEN

Mick's Turn

I SAW THE WHOLE thing. Even from across the street, I could see Boot's look of horror when he was caught. His whole body seemed to crumple in on itself.

He got what he deserved, and I got my revenge.

So why don't I feel great?

Maybe it's the leftover burn from hearing that Tabitha's been taking bets on our fights. Then there's the news that was even worse—that Tabitha said my kiss turned her stomach. *Was that why she didn't stay longer with me under the bridge that afternoon?* But since then, she's acted as if she likes me.

So what's going on?

Of course, it's possible that she never said anything about our making out in the first place. Boot Quinn is perfectly capable of making up nasty lies.

So how do I know who to trust?

I don't feel like going home, so I turn toward the library. I want to see Laura's friendly face. And I have to try to clean the paint off the statue. I hope it'll come off.

A half block from the library, I can see that the statue isn't there. I come closer. The splattered red paint is dry on the cement walkway in front of the door. And the paint is still on the bricks and where it slid down the wall onto the grass. It frames the place where the statue stood. It looks like the scene of a murder.

I guess part of me *did* die, a little connection to Nana. She always seemed closer when I came to the library and saw the statue. But she doesn't feel close today.

A dark mood settles over me. I feel heavy again. But I force myself to pull open the glass library door and walk inside.

Laura is sitting at the circulation desk, staring off into space.

"Hey," I say.

She turns to me, and she looks very upset. "Did you hear what happened?"

I feign ignorance. "What?"

She looks different today. Her face is distorted by anger. Her eyes are cloudy, and her voice is tight.

"The statue," she says. "Some jerk came during the night

and dumped red paint all over the statue and the library wall. Didn't you notice?"

"Yeah," I say. "I wondered what happened."

I can't look at her. I'm shaky, like I'll break down any second and confess that I was the jerk. I want to tell her that I'll scrub off the paint, that I'll do anything to make it right.

But I'm a coward. I don't want her to hate me. I can never explain that I did it to save face because I was dared to—and because I wanted to impress a girl.

"Does anyone know if the paint will come off?" I ask.

"They're going to try using some special solvent," Laura says. She turns to me. "I don't understand what people get out of wrecking something beautiful." I don't answer. "Or doing other selfish things . . . like creating a virus that damages people's computers. Or stealing or . . . even just yanking a clothes hook off a door in the bathroom. What do they *get* out of it?"

"I don't know," I say. It comes out as a whisper.

"Don't they have *lives*? Are they so empty that they have to find a way to make themselves feel powerful? Is that it? Does splashing paint on a work of art make a person feel like he has *power*?"

No. Take it from the voice of experience.

But I don't say it. Instead, I say, "I could try using the cleaner on the library wall. Want me to give it a try?"

"Thanks, Mick, but somebody's already been given that

job. He went to get the stuff at the hardware store."

"Okay," I say. Laura turns away to do some work.

I stroll over and pretend to check out the new books display near the door. After a minute or so, I leave and walk home.

Mom is in the kitchen, rummaging through the refrigerator.

"Hi," I say. "Any word from Dad?"

"No." She pulls out an onion and *thunks* it on the counter. She wheels around and stalks to the pantry and grabs a box of pasta.

"We're having lasagna?" I ask.

"Yup." She yanks a cutting board out of a cabinet and slams it on the counter. Her jaw is set hard.

I dare to ask: "Even though it's Dad's favorite, and he's not—"

"*That's the idea.*" It comes out pretty loud. She grabs a large chef's knife out of a drawer and cuts off the top and root ends of the onion. "I'm not catering to him anymore, Mick. *I've had it.* I've just decided. Tomorrow I'm looking for an apartment for us." She throws the end pieces in the garbage under the sink and slams the door shut.

My mouth opens, but nothing comes out.

She heaves all her strength into chopping that onion. I hope she doesn't lop off one of her fingers.

"Mom?"

"*What?*" She stops and turns to look at me; there's a fire in her eyes.

I wait until the fire's intensity diminishes a tiny bit and ask in a soft voice, "What about Dad?"

"Mick, he'll have to take responsibility for his own life. If he won't stop drinking, I won't take care of him anymore."

"He doesn't cook," I say.

"He can learn," she counters.

"He can't balance a checkbook without screwing up," I say.

She counters me again. "He can keep the calculator."

I'm about to speak, but she holds up her hand and counts on fingers: "He can get an alarm clock, he can learn to operate the washing machine and the iron, and he can pay his own bills."

"But you know he won't," I say.

She levels her gaze. "It's up to him. He can be responsible and grow strong, or he can wither on the vine. It's his life to live; it's his choice."

This woman is an imposter. I've never seen Mom like this. She always tries to keep some kind of peace at home. Seeing her acting strong and angry and taking a stand is kind of disorienting. Like somebody in my brain is stirring up a bubbling brew of confusion; the steam is rising and clouding my vision.

"I've been talking to a counselor," she says.

Aha. With that, she extinguishes the fire under the brew, and my brain begins to clear.

"Okay." I haven't forgotten what she said about their marriage being fourteen years long, but now doesn't seem to be the time to bring it up. After all, she's holding a knife.

"So where are you going to look for an apartment?" I ask.

"I'll look in the paper; I'll find us something."

She goes back to whacking away at the onion.

"Be careful with that weapon," I say.

I turn, walk to my room, and close the door.

Mom and I eat in silence at the dining room table. I wonder if she can even taste the lasagna she made. I realize when mine is nearly gone, I'd hardly thought about the meal. When I finish, I get up and say "Thanks. It was good."

She reaches over and rests a hand on my arm.

"We can do this, Mick," she says. "I'll find us an apartment tomorrow. We'll be okay."

But Dad won't be okay. I don't say it.

"I know," I tell her and take my plate to the kitchen.

After my homework is done, I read for a while. I don't know how some people can go through life without reading. Tonight I don't want to think about anything, especially Mom and Dad. And the statue. And Tabitha.

Yes, Tabitha. I don't know what's going on with her, and

thinking about her just makes me feel bad.

So I plunge back into my Dean Koontz novel. A lot of his books are very funny, and even though my life is a mess, I actually catch myself laughing out loud.

When I get sleepy, I strip to my underwear and crawl into bed. Sleep can sometimes be the best escape there is.

This particular escape only lasts until a little after 2:00 A.M. when I'm startled awake.

"Geddup, Mick."

I jerk up in bed and look around, adrenaline surging through my body.

"What?"

I'm disoriented. The light down the hall in the living room is on, and my dad's silhouette is framed in the doorway. He flips the wall switch, and the overhead light flashes on in my room.

"You heard me," he says. "Get outta bed."

His words are slurred, and he sounds angry. I can't see him very well, because my eyes are squinting in the bright light.

"What's wrong?" I ask, holding a hand up to block the glare.

"I've had enough of your excuses. If you'd work harder, you could play any sport there is. You got the Sullivan genes. Now, geddup."

I don't move fast enough for him, and he grabs my arm and yanks on it.

"I'm gonna make a man out of you yet." He drags me out of bed and pushes me down. "Hit the floor."

"Okay," I say. Now I'm on my knees, and I look up at him.

"Push-ups. Fifty of 'em. Get started."

Fifty push-ups? I'm not sure I can do ten.

"Dad—"

He shoves my shoulder with his foot. "No excuses. Get going."

I start the push-ups.

"One. Two. Three." He's counting them off.

I know I can't do fifty. I also know I'm stronger than he is, and it doesn't take a lot of strength to overpower a drunk man. But I don't want to fight him.

"Four. Five. Six."

"What's going on?" It's Mom. She's in the room now; I can see the hem of her robe and her pink slippers.

"Seven. Eight."

I'm slowing down. My arms are already getting tired.

"Herb!" Now Mom sounds angry. "What are you doing?"

"Nine. Mick's going to toughen up. He's not going to be a sissy-boy anymore. Starting right now. Ten."

"Herb, stop it! Mick, *stop it*!"

She reaches down and grabs my shoulders.

"You stay outta this," Dad yells.

He shoves her, and she lets go of me. Her back hits the door frame. She cries out in pain and slides to the floor. I lunge at Dad and knock him over. He lands on the floor with a thud, and I scramble on top of him and pin his arms.

"*Leave her alone!*" I scream in his face. "*And don't you ever touch her again!*"

He struggles under me, but I don't let him up.

"You hear me?" I yell. "You're a worthless—"

"Mick," Mom yells. She pulls at me. "I'm okay. Let him up."

"You hear me?" I yell again, but he doesn't answer. "*Do. You. Hear. Me?*"

Dad stops struggling. He nods. "Yeah." He says it quietly.

I let a second pass. Two seconds. After three, I let go of his arms.

Mom backs away out of his reach, and I stand up, ready for whatever happens.

He sits up, grunting with the effort. He gets up on his wobbly legs, without saying a word, without looking at Mom or me. He takes in a breath, turns, and shuffles off down the hall to his bedroom.

Mom looks at me and says, "Tomorrow we'll find an apartment. I'll look in the paper."

I nod. She pushes her hands into the pockets of her robe and heads back into the living room.

She'll sleep on the couch tonight, like she has dozens of times before.

CHAPTER NINETEEN

Boot's Turn

I DON'T SLEEP VERY good that night. I keep hoping I'll wake up and find out that Mick's dare was just a bad dream. But I roll over to look at the clock, and it's only an hour later than the last time I checked. And I know it wasn't a dream.

After Mr. Bramer told me and Jesse to come back in the store, he took us in the back room and told me to sit down. Jesse left the door open, so he could see if any customers were out there. The guy who bought the clarinet reeds had already gone.

"Why, Boot?" he asked me. "You just saved the store from a burglar. And now you're stealing from us?" He was quiet a second. "Do you want to play the flute?"

"No."

I couldn't look at Mr. B. His voice sounded sad. If he'd

sounded mad, I could have taken it better.

"So what were you going to do with it?" Jesse said. "Sell it?"

"No."

"You having a problem?" Mr. B. asked. "You need money?"

"You need *drug* money?" Jesse sounded really mad. "Is that it?"

I looked up at that. "*No,*" I told him. I didn't want him to think I was on drugs. Jesse hates it when musicians are using. He always says they're throwing away their talent.

"I was going to give it back," I said.

"Oh, yeah, *right.*"

I didn't blame Jesse for not believing me. It sounded so lame.

"It was stupid, I know," I said. "It was a dare. Just a stupid dare."

"Somebody dared you to steal from us?" Mr. B. asked, frowning.

"Yeah."

"Boot, you know I should call the police," he said.

"*I was going to give it back,*" I tell him.

Jesse let out a snort. "And that's supposed to make it all right?"

"Jesse, will you go out and look after the store?" Mr. B. said.

"Yeah, I need to get away from *him*." He turned around and walked back into the store and slammed the door behind him.

I was starting to feel sick.

"Boot," Mr. B. said. "I still can't conceive of why you'd steal from us. But I think you'll understand why I have to tell you not to come back here anymore."

I felt my eyes filling up, and I stared at the floor, willing the tears not to spill out, willing my stomach not to throw up.

"I'm not going to call the police," Mr. B. said. "And I'm not going to call your dad. I know things aren't easy for you at home."

How did he know about that?

"But you can't come to the store anymore," he went on. "*Ever.* If I see you here, I *will* call the police."

I couldn't believe this was happening, that my two favorite people were turning on me. This was a nightmare.

If it only *was* a nightmare. But it really happened. And now my friends aren't my friends.

I wake up again at eight in the morning when the phone rings. I know Ethan and Dad will be mad about somebody calling so early. They're not usually out of bed on Saturday until at least ten. I grab it before it rings a second time.

"Hello?"

"Hey, Boot. It's Tab."

Tabitha.

"Hey," I say. I don't really want to talk to her.

"So what happened?" she asks. "I've been dying to talk to you, but my parents made me go to my aunt's stupid birthday party last night, and I couldn't get away to call."

"Oh. Well, I stole a flute."

"Yeah, and that guy caught you! We saw all that. What happened after he made you go inside? You knew him, right? He's a friend?"

"Yeah," I said. "He was."

"So did you tell him it was just a dare?"

"Yeah. But it didn't make any difference."

"It didn't? Did he call the cops?"

"No."

"*Really?* Why not? Because you were the one who caught that robber? He felt like he owed you or something? Or was it because you guys were friends?"

"I don't know. Uh, Tabitha? I really can't talk now."

"Oh."

"I—I got to go help my dad."

"Oh," she says again. "Sure. Well, maybe you can call me back later?"

"Maybe. I don't know."

"Okay."

I hang up and lie back in bed. I wish I could fall asleep again. I'd like to be like that guy who sleeps for a hundred years. Or maybe just until I'm eighteen or something. Then

I could get away from here and get a job. Do something different. Maybe join a band and go on tour.

If I got famous, maybe Jesse and Mr. B. would come to a concert and come backstage and shake my hand. And we could be friends again.

I know my brain is too busy and my body's too awake to go back to sleep. I put on my headphones and listen to a CD. I close my eyes and picture myself playing guitar with a stadium full of screaming and dancing people.

Dad and Ethan get up later and say they're going car shopping. They decided they want a new Mustang, and that sounds good to me. We pile into Dad's old Chevy and head to the Ford dealer. It's cloudy, and before we get two blocks from home, it starts drizzling.

Ethan has looked at the Mustangs online, and he's talking a lot more than usual, doing a sales pitch on my dad.

"These Mustangs are cool," he says. "They got the lines of the old fastbacks. The GTs can really kick butt—three-hundred-horsepower engines, and they can do zero to sixty in five point one seconds. And they got three-hundred-twenty-pound feet of torque. So I bet if you added two turbochargers and higher rear-end gear, they could do two hundred."

"Miles an hour?" I ask from the backseat.

"You won't be doing two hundred in *my* car," Dad says.

"But you *could*," Ethan tells him.

"Not in *my* car."

That shuts Ethan up. Fat raindrops are hitting the windshield. I watch one and see if I can hold my breath till it runs down the glass. It's pretty easy, so I do that with another drop higher on the window.

We turn into the Ford lot and get out of the car. It's not raining hard, and we start looking around at all the cars.

Ethan says he sees one he likes and leads us to this cool-looking red Mustang. He opens the driver's door and sits behind the wheel on the leather seat. I lean in. Dad stands behind me.

"Leather-wrapped wheel," Ethan says, trying out the feel of it under his hands. "See the round analog dials?" He points at the dash, but Dad doesn't move. "They look like they did in the sixties. And you can backlight those dials in just about any color you want."

"Cool interior," I say.

Ethan points. "CD player."

Dad looks at the sticker on the window and scowls. "They sure don't cost sixties prices."

Ethan scowls up at him. "You can't expect to pay sixties prices."

"Remember, this is *my* car," Dad says.

Ethan turns in the seat to look back at Dad. "You're going to let me drive it, though, aren't you?"

"I dunno," Dad says. "With all your big talk about two hundred miles an hour—"

"I was just saying what it *can* go," Ethan says. "I'm not going out drag racing."

A sales guy walks over. "Morning," he says.

Dad nods but doesn't say anything.

"That's the most popular car on the lot," the guy says, smiling. "Have you ever driven a Mustang?"

"Long time ago," Dad answers.

"Well, if you want to take it for a drive, you're in for a treat. I'm Jim Means." The guy holds out his hand.

Dad shakes it. "Yeah, we'll take it for a drive."

The guy gets us the keys. I wonder who will drive first, but Ethan's smart and doesn't say anything when Dad takes the keys and gets into the driver's seat. Ethan takes the front seat on the passenger side, and I get in back.

Dad turns the ignition and revs it a few times. It sounds like a race car, then settles down to a smooth purr.

Ethan half smiles. "V-eight engine. *Sweet.*"

We drive to the lot entrance and out into the street.

"Are we gonna buy this car?" I ask.

"You can get some great options," Ethan tells Dad. "Like a thousand-watt audio system with two subwoofers in the front doors. And premium speakers in back. And a six-disc CD changer with MP-three capability."

My dad swears. "Just how much money do you think I have?"

Ethan looks mad. "I just told you what we *could* get."

"What *I* could get." Dad's voice is loud. "This is *my* car. I got the raise."

Ethan mutters something under his breath that I can't hear, but I'm pretty sure Dad does because he slams on the brakes.

"Get out," Dad says.

"*What?*" Ethan looks like he can't believe it. "You're throwing me out of the car? It's *raining*, and I'm—"

"You're lucky I'm not gonna knock your head off."

"Oh, great," Ethan says. "Just *great*." He gets out of the car, slams the door shut, and starts walking away.

My dad guns the engine and we roar off, tires squealing.

I look out the back window at Ethan standing on the street in the rain. He stops and holds up his hand. We're too far away to see the finger, but I'm sure it's there, standing tall and proud, in case my dad decides to look in the rearview mirror.

We don't get the car.

CHAPTER TWENTY

Mick's Turn

IT RAINED ALL weekend, fitting weather for my mood. Dad slept through most of it, and Mom went out to find an apartment. I was too depressed to go with her, so I stayed home and read.

The phone rang while she was gone, and I checked the Caller ID. No surprise—it said LOUIS SLATER, from Tabitha's house. I didn't pick it up. She didn't leave a message. About a half hour later, she called back and didn't leave a message that time, either. I knew she wanted to talk about the dare I gave Boot, but I didn't have the energy to talk.

Mom came home and said she'd found a two-bedroom apartment over on Macey Road. It's still on the north side, so I'll keep going to the same school.

I asked her when she was going to tell Dad about it. She gave me some vague answer about playing it by ear.

* * *

Monday morning brings rain, so I wear my hooded poncho to school. On the way, I try to think of something in my life that isn't depressing. So I fantasize about four years from now when I can leave this town and go to college. But that's so far away, I get even more depressed.

It doesn't take more than the first fifteen minutes at school to find out that everyone knows about the dare I gave Boot. I hear comments about it all morning.

"Hey, Mick! You really showed Boot!"

"I wonder if he'll be at school today. Have you seen him?"

"I hear the cops arrested Boot. Will you testify at his trial?"

"He'll be so mad that he'll come after you! Be sure to let me know if he says he's going to fight you." (And no, that one didn't come from Tabitha. Or any of her minions.)

And finally, "What's up next with you guys? How're you going to top *that*?"

I don't have the energy to come up with smart-ass remarks today, so I just shrug or mutter some non-answer like "I dunno" or "Yeah, sure."

I operate on autopilot through most of the morning and walk down the hall to the game room at eleven, not caring what happens. Good or bad, it doesn't matter. I'm sick of the game room, sick of Boot, and sick of Tabitha. And my dad. I'm pretty much sick of my life in general.

When I get to the main office, Boot's already there. I collapse into a chair three down from where he's sitting. He doesn't look at me, and his face doesn't give me a hint about what happened at River City Music after he was caught. He sits with his arms folded loosely across his chest and stares at the far wall.

Mrs. Taylor looks up at us and nods in the direction of the game room. "Go on back."

I sigh and stand up. Boot gets up, too, and plods along behind me. I sit on the couch, and Boot falls into the big chair. He stares at the floor and doesn't speak.

A minute passes. "What do you say we call a truce?" I say.

I hadn't planned on asking him. It just came into my head, and I said it.

"We can call a truce, but I still hate you," he says without looking at me.

"I can live with that," I tell him. He's still staring at the wall. "So did anyone call the police?"

"No."

Silence. *So what happened?* I want to ask. But I don't. Instead, I say, "What game do you want to play?"

"I don't care."

"I don't, either. How about Scrabble?"

He shrugs, so I open the box. I wonder if he knows how

to play Scrabble. If he does, he should know that I'll cream him.

I set one of the little wooden racks in front of him. He looks at it and at all the tiles with letters on them, and something comes into his eyes. I think he remembers that this is a word-building game.

His face doesn't change, but he picks up the rack and throws it across the room. It hits the wall, and clatters down into the space between the desk and the wall.

"I take it you changed your mind about Scrabble."

He doesn't answer.

I don't want to play a game anyway. I'm tired.

I get up and walk to the desk. It's made of a heavy wood, so it's not light. I pull it away from the wall and squat down to look for the rack on the floor.

But I find something more interesting. It's a small door in the wall, about three feet high and three feet wide.

"What's this?"

I pull the desk farther away. A piece of wood is nailed to the door frame with one nail and turned so that it blocks the door from being opened from the other side. I turn the piece of wood and pull a small knob on the door.

At first it doesn't open. But I pull harder, and it finally swings toward me, dust puffing into my face. I wave my hand and wait a few seconds for the dust to settle so I can see.

Just beyond the door is a dark space going down.

I peer into the dark, but I can't see what's down there. Just below the door is a ladder that descends into the murk.

I hear footsteps and glance over to see that Boot has come up behind me.

"I'm going down," I tell him.

"What's down there?"

I look up at him. "How would I know?"

He scowls, and I slide my feet and legs into the space. My feet find the ladder rungs, and I lower myself into the space.

The top of the tunnel is about three feet over my head. And it's probably not quite six feet wide.

I wait for my eyes to get more accustomed to the dark.

Boot is watching me from above.

"I can't see much," I tell him. "But it has concrete walls." I scuff my feet. "And a cement floor that probably hasn't been cleaned since the school was built."

"When was that?"

"This part of the school—maybe in the sixties."

I run my hand over the wall under the ladder, and it pushes through a wispy tangle of spiderwebs.

"Spiders," I say. "Which means there could be other things living down here, too."

"Like rats."

I look up the ladder, expecting to see a smirk on Boot's face. But he's just peering into the space, looking serious.

"Anything crunching under your shoes?" he asks.

"No, but I'm standing still. Why?"

"If there are rats down there," he says, "you'll step on dried rat turds."

I stare up at him. "Thanks for sharing." He looks mad. "Boot, I'm kidding. If there are rats down here, don't you think I'd want to know? And the only source of dried rat turds that I can think of is from dried rats. Or possibly fresh, non-dried rats."

What I don't say is that I'm very nervous about rats. My mom grew up on a farm, and she told me about rats that can grow as big as cats. She said when they're cornered, they stand up on their hind legs and bare their teeth, ready to fight. I'm all for hands-on education, but I draw the line at rats.

"Say, you don't happen to have a flashlight on you, do you?" I ask.

Boot's eyes narrow. "I gave away my last one on the way to school."

I smile. "See? You don't have to answer every one of my smart-ass remarks with an insult. Just deflect it with a smart-ass remark of your own. Doesn't it feel good?"

He doesn't answer my question. "Can't you see anything? Hey, wait a minute."

He fishes in his pockets and comes up with a cigarette lighter.

"Oh, yeah." I remembered seeing him with a cigarette

that night at the library. "You smoke."

"I'm coming down," he says.

He slides his legs into the tunnel and climbs down the ladder.

"So how often do you smoke?" I ask him.

He shrugs. "Whenever I feel like it."

"You really *are* an idiot."

"Maybe," he says. "But I'm the idiot with the lighter. So get out of my way."

I can't help but laugh. I step aside. He flicks on the lighter and holds it up. We both peer into the darkness.

The tiny flame only brightens a few yards in front of us. I can see boxes on the floor, a bucket, and an old mop.

But beyond the part we can see is more darkness.

"Unless this is a very long, narrow room, I'd say we're in a tunnel," I tell him. "I wonder how far it goes."

"There's only one way to find out."

I stare at him. He looks kind of excited.

"Okay," I tell him. "You've got the lighter, so you lead the way. If any rats *are* down here, they'll tear *you* apart first."

That stops him for a second. He scowls and then starts walking. I follow close behind, listening for the skittering sound of little rat feet.

CHAPTER TWENTY-ONE

Boot's Turn

THE TUNNEL IS scary because we can't see very far, and we don't know what's down here. Lots of junk is piled up on both sides: wooden desks that kids probably used a long time ago, rusty file cabinets, old fluorescent lights, stacks of boxes, and some other stuff. Over our heads are pipes running along the ceiling. I hear a gurgling sound. They must be water pipes.

It's weird that the school has a tunnel underneath, and nobody knows about it. At least I don't think any *kids* know about it. So even though it's scary, it's also kind of cool to be down here exploring.

Even though I have to do it with Mick.

I still hate him. I don't know why he asked if I want to call a truce. Maybe he thinks I was spooked because I got caught stealing. But I'll never give him the satisfaction of knowing it got to me.

Anyway, right now, I want to see what's down here. I figure we'd better do it pretty quick because if we're caught, they'll make sure we never come down again. And besides, it's really cold.

I walk in front and pretty slow, so I can see what's here as we go by. I hope rats don't live down here.

Mick must have been thinking the same thing, because he says, "How do you know so much about dried rat turds?"

"I *don't* know a lot about dried rat turds," I say.

"I mean, the crunch factor."

"What?"

"I mean, the fact that they crunch under your feet."

"My uncle bought this abandoned house a few years ago," I tell him. "The place was crammed with rats."

"Crammed, hunh?"

He's making fun of me again. I stop and turn to him. "If you ever wonder why I hate you so much, just listen to yourself. You act like you're so much better than me."

He grins. "That's because I *am* better than you."

"You're such a jerk," I tell him.

"Boot," he says. "Can't you take a joke? I'm just kidding."

"Kidding on the square."

"Kidding on the square? What do you mean?"

"You said 'because I *am* better than you.' Now you say you're only joking, but you meant it. That's how people like you try to get away with insulting people. When somebody calls you on it, you . . . like . . . dance away, pretending you were joking. It's kidding on the square. It's a game you play a lot."

"Kidding on the square." He stares at me a second, then he nods. "Very astute of you."

He says that like maybe it's a compliment, but I don't trust him. I memorize the word, so I can look it up later and decide whether to punch him for it.

I turn and start walking again. I wonder how far the tunnel goes. And how often anyone comes down here. It doesn't look like it's very often. Everything looks real old and dirty, and there's heavy dust covering all the junk.

My thumb that's holding down the plastic thing on the lighter is getting tired. But I know the wheel that you spin to relight it is real hot by now. So I transfer the lighter to my other hand.

A sound like whooshing water runs through the pipes over our heads.

"Someone must've flushed a toilet," Mick says.

I don't say anything.

"Just thought you'd like a news alert," he says.

I ignore him.

"I wonder if there's another entrance to the tunnel," he says.

"There has to be," I tell him.

"Why?"

"Because some of this stuff is too big to go through the door we used."

"Well, Boot Quinn," he says. "You *do* have a brain in there somewhere."

"Shut up."

"Wouldn't it be cool to find a door that opens to a classroom? And we'd pop in and say hello? We'd get our butts suspended, but it'd be worth it. Wouldn't you love to see all those astonished faces?"

I don't answer.

"Or maybe we'd open the door," he says, "and we'd be in the girls' locker room."

This time I laugh. "That'd be cool."

I'm starting to imagine which girls might be having gym when he says, "Boot?"

"What?"

"Did you know that Tabitha's taking bets on our fights? She and her friends are betting on who wins."

I stop and look at him again. "What are you talking about?"

"She keeps score on the locker-room wall. She's making money on our fights. And all the girls are keeping track."

I shrug. "Yeah, so?"

Mick's face on the other side of my lighter flame stares hard at me.

"You don't care?" he asks.

"What difference does it make?"

"She's using us," he says.

I shrug again. "No, she's not. I'd fight you anyway."

"Well, yeah, but . . ." His voice fades away. "Hmm. I guess I'd fight you anyway, too."

I roll my eyes and start walking again.

After a few seconds, I ask, "So who's winning?"

"You mean, you or me?"

"Yeah."

"We were running neck and neck, so it depends on whether they counted the dares as fights," Mick says. "They really should. The dares are more imaginative than fights."

Mick's probably the only guy for a hundred miles who'd rather be known for imagination than for being tough.

"No crunching under my feet," Mick says. "So maybe the worst living things down here are spiders."

"No, right now, the worst living thing down here is *you*," I say.

Mick lets out a laugh. "Hey, Boot, that was good. And quick! You're really *not* as dumb as you look."

I pretend I don't hear that. I keep sweeping my lighter back and forth in the dark, but my other thumb is getting tired.

My foot comes down on something crunchy, and I lower the lighter to see what's on the tunnel floor.

"Rat turd," I say.

"*Really?*" He sounds scared. "Are you sure?"

"Aren't your feet crunching?"

"No." He takes a step and makes a gasping noise. "*Yes. Let's get out of here.*"

"Wait." I lean over, holding the lighter near the floor and look around. "If a lot of rats are down here, we'd see *lots* of turds, and the boxes and stuff would all be chewed on. Maybe somebody got rid of the rats years ago. Or maybe they just started getting into the tunnel recently."

I can hear Mick's breathing, and it's pretty fast. "Well, we're not the welcoming party, so I'm leaving," he says.

"Don't you want to see where the tunnel goes?" I ask.

I move a box to make more room, and a skittering thing runs over my shoe.

"*Oh, geez!*" Mick turns, bolts back to the ladder, and hurries up.

I hold out the lighter and look into the shadows.

"Come on," he calls out from the top of the ladder. He sounds out of breath.

"It wasn't a rat," I yell at him.

"Spiders don't run like that," he says.

"It ran over *your* shoe, too?"

"Yeah. *Why are you still down there?*"

I walk back to the ladder and look up at him. "It wasn't a rat. Just a little brown mouse. I can hear it squeaking."

"I don't care how big a rodent it is. I'm not going back down there."

I laugh, and he looks embarrassed. But I realize that he could slam the door shut, turn the piece of wood, and I'd be stuck down here in the cold with nothing but my lighter.

So I climb up into the game room.

At noon, we go to the caf to get our lunches. Everybody's watching us. They know I got caught shoplifting Friday at River City—they were all talking about it this morning.

Sullivan and I go through the lunch line, and as I'm walking across the caf to leave, J.K. comes up and stops me.

"Hey, man, how'd it go after you were caught at the music store? Did you get arrested?"

Mick keeps walking and goes out the caf door.

"No," I say.

"So are you gonna get Sullivan back?"

Tabitha and Cheyanne hurry over. "Hey, Boot, how are ya?" Tabitha asks.

"Okay."

Over Tabitha's shoulder, I can see lots of people watching us.

"So are you gonna get him back?" J.K. asks again.

Tabitha and Cheyanne lean in to hear what I say.

"Maybe," I tell them.

"*Maybe?*" J.K. says. "You gotta stomp on him for that."

"How come the music store guy didn't call the cops?" Tabitha asks.

"He didn't?" says J.K. "How come?"

I'm not sure why Mr. Bramer didn't call the cops. But I still don't feel like talking about it. Every time I even think about that stupid dare, I feel horrible.

"I don't know," I say. I shrug and take a step backward. "I really don't know." I take another step. "I don't know."

I turn and walk out of the caf and back to the game room. Mick is sitting on the couch, leaning over his lunch on the coffee table.

I sit on the chair and put my tray across my knees. I'm sitting sort of sideways, so I'm not facing him.

"Chicken nuggets," Mick says. He stabs two on a fork and crams them in his mouth.

We eat for a while. When Mick's done, he shoves his tray to the side and wipes his mouth with his napkin.

"So what happened at River City after Mr. Bramer and his son stopped you on the sidewalk?"

I glare over at him. "How do you know their name?"

He sits back on the couch. "I played the trumpet in fifth and sixth grades, and Mr. Bramer let us buy it in installments. He's a nice guy."

I look away. I haven't finished my nuggets, but I don't want them.

"Was he nice to you yesterday?"

"None of your business." Then I realize that he didn't ask it sarcastically, or like J.K. and Tabitha did, like he was waiting to hear the worst parts. "Yeah. He was nice."

"You were an idiot to take the dare."

I open my mouth to tell him where to go, but before I can say it, he says, "As big an idiot as I was to take yours." He sort of smiles. "Let's face it, we're a couple of idiots."

"At least, I'm not an idiot who's scared of mice."

He laughs and throws a carrot stick at me. I duck.

Then I throw a celery stick at him.

And that's pretty much how we ended our lunch. With a carrot-and-celery-stick fight.

CHAPTER TWENTY-TWO

Mick's Turn

AFTER SCHOOL, TABITHA appears at my locker.

"Hey, Mick," she says.

"Hey," I say. I'm pulling books off the shelf that I need for homework.

"Are you mad at me?" She's smiling up at me with her head tipped at an angle.

"No." And I'm not. But all those planes are grounded and off the runway. Nobody's flying today.

I'm surprised. Not that they're not flying, but I'm surprised that I don't care that they're not flying.

"So, what was it like in the game room today?" she asks. "I mean, after Boot got caught stealing at River City. Was he really mad?"

"We didn't talk about it much," I tell her.

"Really? I saw him at lunch, and he didn't seem all that

mad. I just wondered what was going on with you guys."

I shrug and close my locker door.

"Not much," I tell her. "Well . . . see you."

I nod and walk away. She's still standing there at my locker, and I hear her say "Okay" in a soft voice.

If anyone had told me a week ago that I'd be walking away from Tabitha Slater and not really caring about talking to her, I would've said they were out of their mind.

It's weird what can happen in a week.

When I get home, Mom and Dad are sitting at the dining room table. The space between them is nearly buzzing, there's so much tension in the air.

I stop in the doorway; I don't want to get closer. The nervousness in my body stiffens me. They look up.

"Hey," I say.

"Mick," Dad says. "I'm sorry for my behavior the other night."

I never know how much Dad remembers after he sleeps it off. Does he remember making me do push-ups? And shoving Mom? And how I knocked him on the floor and held down his arms?

Puddles are standing in dad's eyes. It's not the first time I've seen that, but it always gets to me.

"It's okay," I say.

"No, it's not," he says. "Please forgive me. Don't move

out, Mick. I promised your mom it'll never happen again."

He's said it a hundred times before. His promises don't mean anything anymore, but we always hope he'll be sorry enough this time to stay sober.

I look at Mom. Her eyes are red, but she shakes her head at me.

What do I say? I love them both. When I was five and they argued, I'd run to my room and crawl under the covers. I still have the urge to run out. Out of the room, out of the house, out of this town. It doesn't matter where. I just want to get away.

Mom does the talking for me.

"Herb, Mick and I will be six blocks away. We'll see you any time you're sober. We love you, but we won't live with you anymore." She looks up at me now. "Your dad lost his job."

She doesn't say *again.* He's had more jobs than I can count.

Dad starts to cry again. "Please. I know I don't deserve it, but please give me one more chance." He turns to me. "Mick . . ."

I close my eyes, so I don't have to look at him.

"Mick," Mom says, "I think it'll be good for Dad to live on his own for now. He'll get another job and deal with living on his own for a while."

"I can't be in the middle of this," I say. I open my eyes

and look at Mom and then at Dad. "Both of you—leave me out of this discussion. I can't choose between you."

"You're not coming with me?" Mom asks.

"Don't leave, Mick." Dad is pleading; he's had a lot of practice, and he's very good at it. "I promise, son. It'll never happen again."

"Just leave me alone, okay?" I say to them both. "I need some time to think."

I turn and walk through the kitchen, down the hall, and into my bedroom.

I sit in my desk chair and stare out the window.

I don't want to think about this. They're making me decide, and I don't want to choose.

If I leave, Dad will be lost. He can't function without Mom. He's not responsible about tending to the details of life, so she does everything for him. She has to, so the bills get paid, so we have insurance, so we eat decent meals. Mom and I do the laundry, vacuum the house, paint the walls when they need it, pull the weeds out of the garden, and see to the repairs when something goes wrong.

Dad and I mow the grass and shovel the snow. I do it alone when he's on a binge or sleeping it off.

He *does* work to earn a living. When he can keep a job, anyway.

But Mom works nearly full-time, too.

I sit back in the chair and drum my fingers on the desk.

The book that Laura gave me at the library last week sits next to my hand. *Games People Play*, by Eric Berne, M.D. I'd been finishing the Koontz novel, so I didn't get to it yet.

If I read, I don't have to think. I pick the book up, take it over to my bed, open it, and begin reading.

Turns out Laura was right. It's about how people play games to get what they want.

I come to a game called Alcoholic.

I read about that game, and realize I'm reading about Dad, Mom, and me.

Dad, of course, plays the Alcoholic. Mom and I are the Dummies when we do all the work and take care of his life, so he doesn't have to be responsible for himself. She's also the Persecutor, who scolds him in the morning when he wakes up, and the Rescuer when she makes him promise to stop drinking.

And the game is played over and over.

The more I read, the more I realize that the best thing Mom and I can do is refuse to play the game.

That's what Mom's doing by moving out.

I close the book and then close my eyes. I'm getting sleepy; I'll tell her when I wake up that I'll move out with her. I don't want to think about how Dad will react.

My brain gets fuzzy, and I float into sleep.

* * *

I see Boot on the way to school the next day. He's by himself, loping along the sidewalk on the other side of the street.

"Hey, Boot," I call out.

He looks over and sees me. He doesn't answer and keeps walking.

His hair is wet, as usual, but this time I don't say anything about it.

I look up at the blue sky. It's one of those days in September when the sun is warm, but the cool breeze whispers a friendly warning that summer is fading fast.

Since I made the decision to stop playing the game with Dad and to move out with Mom, I've realized that we should have done that a long time ago. It feels good that I've made the decision. I still don't want to think about Dad. But maybe if he realizes his safety net is gone, he'll stop walking the tightrope.

I told Mom about my decision last night, but I didn't have the courage to tell Dad yet.

I watch Boot. He has kind of a *galumph* to his stride.

"Nice day, hunh?" I call out to him.

Either he doesn't hear me or he is ignoring me, so I cross the street and walk alongside him. His nose is red.

"What do *you* want?" he growls. He sounds stuffed up, like he has a cold.

"Nothing," I tell him. "I just thought if we call a truce,

we could really create some gossip."

He doesn't look at me but says, "Why would I want to do that?"

"Oh, you know, keep 'em on their toes, that sort of thing. They won't be able to stand it. They'll all wonder what they missed. Want to?"

"No," he says.

But he doesn't call me names, so I figure that's a positive sign.

"If everybody thinks we suddenly don't hate each other anymore," I say, "Tabitha will be calling us all hours of the day and night, trying to get the story. Hey, do you think she eats gossip like food? Maybe that's the energy that keeps her going."

"You're an idiot," he says.

Okay, so he calls me a name. Big deal. I get grumpy when I have a cold, too.

"Guess I'll go around to the other door, so you don't have to walk with me and cause a scene on the school grounds," I tell him. "Nice chatting with you, Boot."

"Why don't you go soak your head in a toilet," he says.

I smile. "And *you* have a good day, too."

I notice today that the limelight I've been in is suddenly dimmer than yesterday. People at school look at me in the halls, but they're not calling out to me as much as they did last week.

Oh, I hear an occasional "Hey, Mick!" or "Anything

exciting going on with you and Boot?"

I shake my head, and they disappear.

Fickle folks, that's what they are. Boot and I aren't the hot topic that we were last week. We haven't gotten into fist-fights the last few days, so they don't bother with us. If Boot had gotten arrested for theft, we'd probably still be the favorite topic of gossip.

At eleven o'clock, I go to the principal's office and sit down. Boot's already there, but he doesn't look at me when I sit down two chairs away from him. He sniffs and wipes his nose on his arm.

Mrs. Taylor waves at us to go into the game room.

We meet Mr. Maddox who walks in behind us.

"Boot," he says. "I just heard on the radio this morning that Springsteen's coming to Chicago at the end of the month. Did you know that?"

Boot looks at him and blinks. "Really?"

"You ought to go if you can. My wife and I are going with a few friends."

Boot's face takes on a faraway look. He sniffs and wipes his nose on his sleeve again.

"Have a seat," Mr. Maddox says.

We sit on the couch. He disappears and returns with a box of tissues, which he hands to Boot.

He sits on the chair across the coffee table. "I've been

thinking about our conversation last week about this time in the game room." He turns to me. "Last week you said you didn't think it was helping. Are we wasting our time?"

"Well, no," I say. "It's not a total waste."

"What are you getting out of it?" he asks.

"You mean, other than getting out of class?"

He gazes at me steadily. "Yes, Mick, other than getting out of class."

"Well, I've gotten to know Boot, sort of."

"And what have you learned about him?" he asks.

"What have I learned?"

"Yeah." He smiles a little. "What good things have you found out about Boot?"

"Good things? Oh . . ." I poke around in my mind, looking for something good to say.

I've learned that Boot is good at cheating.

He's good at bad sportsmanship.

He's great at getting caught shoplifting.

But I have a feeling that's not the kind of answer he has in mind.

So I think for another few seconds and say, "Boot's pretty smart."

Boot stares at me from his side of the couch, but his eyes narrow, and I can tell he's suspicious.

Mr. Maddox raises his eyebrows. "Tell me about that."

"I can see him figuring things out while we play. He

plans strategies and then uses them to win."

Now Boot's eyes get huge.

"That's great," he says. "I had a feeling that you're a capable young man, Boot." He nods at Boot. "And what about you? What good things have you learned about Mick?"

Boot looks at me.

"Here's your chance to say something nice back," I tell him.

He says slowly, "Well . . . he's not afraid to let people know he's scared of mice." I groan, and he says, "That takes guts."

Mr. Maddox grins. "That *does* take guts, Mick." Now he laughs. "What game are you playing today?"

"We haven't played checkers yet," I say.

"Okay," he says.

"See you later." Mr. Maddox leaves.

"That's the nicest thing you can say about me?" I ask Boot. "Couldn't you have said, 'he's good looking,' or 'he's brilliant,' or 'he's God's gift to women'?"

He doesn't answer but opens the checkers box and pulls out the board. "I think he goes to lunch just after we do, right?" he says.

"I don't know. Why?"

"So after lunch, I'm going back into the tunnel. I want to see how far it goes."

"Why?" I ask. "It's not like there's anything really cool down there."

He shoves his hand into his jeans pocket and comes up with a small penlight.

"The *tunnel* is cool," he says. He sets up the checker board. "Which color do you want?"

"I don't care," I say.

He shoves the red checkers over to me and starts setting up his side of the board.

"Who's going first?" he asks.

"I don't care. You go."

He moves one of his pieces, then looks up at me.

"So why are you so scared of a little mouse?" he says.

"Because of my mom's stories about gargantuan rats on the farm." I show him how big with my hand. Maybe I exaggerate a tiny bit.

He frowns. "This was a little brown mouse."

I move out one of my checkers. "They spread disease."

"Like what?"

"The plague."

He makes a face. "The *plague*?"

"Well, the mice *would* spread the plague if the plague was a problem." He stares at me. "It killed thousands of people in London."

"When was that?"

"Oh, the late sixteenth century and the mid-seventeenth century."

He rolls his eyes and moves another checker. "You're an idiot."

"You already said that today," I tell him. "And I called *you* an idiot yesterday. Can't you say anything original?"

"I don't want to work that hard," he says. "I'd rather just call you an idiot. Or a wuss, scared of a tiny mouse." He moves another checker.

I sigh. I suspect I'm not going to hear the end of this any time soon.

We play four games of checkers. I beat him three times; he beats me once.

"You're only beating me because I'm thinking about going back down in the tunnel."

"What an excuse," I say.

At noon, we go down to get our lunches.

I can almost hear the yawns as we walk through the caf, the ingrates. We had entertained them all last week, and what do we get now? Just a passing nod or two.

I notice that Tabitha watches us, but she doesn't get up and run over the way she has before.

We go back upstairs and eat. Boot shovels his lunch into his mouth with amazing speed.

"You're ruining my appetite," I tell him.

He pays no attention.

When he's finished eating, he gets up, walks softly to the door, and peeks around the corner.

"The principal's gone. Mrs. Taylor's on the phone. I'm going down there. You coming? Or are you too scared?"

"Boot," I say. I stop, realizing there's no point in denying it. "I'm too scared."

He laughs. "It's a tiny mouse, and you're an elephant!"

"A nicely formed elephant, thank you very much."

He goes to the desk.

"What about our checkers game?" I say.

"You're so smart," he tells me. "Play checkers with yourself. You can switch back and forth on both sides of the board."

"That's no fun," I say. "Maybe I'll sit in the doorway of the tunnel and shout orders at you."

He pulls the desk away from the wall. Then he squats down and pulls open the tunnel door.

I get up, and after he's gone down, I sit in the small doorway with my legs hanging into the tunnel.

Below me, Boot flicks on his penlight and shines it over the tunnel walls.

"It's real dirty down here," he says. He bends down and shines the light over the floor. "I only see a few mouse turds."

"What good news," I say, but it doesn't sound sincere because I didn't *mean* for it to sound sincere. "Shine your light into the depths of the tunnel and see if you can see where it ends."

He holds out the penlight. "I can't see that far." He looks up at me, then pulls the lighter out of his pocket. "Here," he says. "In case you change your mind and want to come down."

He walks to the ladder and hands it up to me.

"See ya, coward," he says.

He turns and moves off deeper into the tunnel until I can't see him or his tiny beam of light.

I sit there feeling pretty stupid about my fear of mice. It's irrational. I mean, if there were *rats* down there as big as cats—that would be one thing. *But mice? Tiny squeaky little mice? What possible harm could they do to me?*

Okay, that's it. I lower myself onto the ladder, ducking my head through the doorway. I can see Boot about thirty feet away, moving around with his penlight.

"Can you see the end yet?" I call out softly to him. I have to keep my voice down so Mrs. Taylor won't hear.

He doesn't answer; he probably doesn't hear me.

I really want to go with him and see where the tunnel ends, so I climb the rest of the way down the ladder and flick on the lighter.

"Boot?"

No answer. I can see him off in the distance. His light looks like Tinkerbell, flittering around in the dark.

I listen. No scurrying mice feet. Just the muffled noise Boot is making as he moves through the tunnel.

This is ridiculous, I tell myself. Mice are more afraid of me than I am of them. Probably.

I start walking, holding the lighter out in front of me. I decide that any mice running across my feet will be completely ignored.

If I can keep myself from screaming.

I've read that affirmations can be very helpful in changing human behavior. I try out an affirmation, which is supposed to be stated as a positive. *"I like mice."* I follow it with a less convincing, *"I'm really fond of rodents."*

What a liar.

But maybe if I say it loud enough, my voice will scare any nearby mice so they'll run away from me.

I walk past a lot of stuff that I saw the last time we were down here. Occasionally I step on something crunchy, which I assume is a dried mouse turd, but I grit my teeth, say my affirmations to myself again, and keep going.

A stack of boxes to my right catches my eye. I hold the lighter a few inches over my head. The top box says OLD BOOKS — LIBRARY on it.

Old novels, maybe? It would be fun to see what kids were reading decades ago. I pull the box down, being careful to hold the flame away from the box. As I'm putting it on the floor, my thumb is bumped off the little plastic thing that keeps the lighter lit; the flame goes out, and darkness rushes in to consume everything. I start to spin the wheel with my thumb to relight it, but it's like putting my thumb on a hot poker.

"*Yeow!*" I drop the lighter, my thumb burned, and it clatters to the floor.

I stand there, my pulse surging, and look around. I'm standing in darkness so black, I can't even see *anything*. I can't see Boot anymore. "Boot!" I yell loudly now. I'm sure Mrs. Taylor won't hear me, and at this point, I don't even care. But Boot's too far away to hear me. If I crouch down and feel around in the dark for the lighter at my feet, I might touch turds—or a *rat*.

Okay, a mouse. But in the dark, it might as well be a rat. *What should I do now? Just don't panic.*

I consider standing here and waiting for Boot to come back. But I'm so creeped out by the total blackness, I decide that waiting is not an option. I extend my foot carefully out a few inches. I don't hit the lighter. I tap my toe in front of me, then start tapping a few inches out and around. After I've completed one circle, I extend the circle wider and continue to tap, searching for the lighter.

I still haven't found it after a minute of trying. So I tap my foot along the side of the box that I put on the floor. And that's when I hit it.

I reach down and tap it with my fingers to make sure I

don't burn my fingers again. I pick it up and flick the striker using the bottom of my shirt. A flame bursts out of the top of the lighter.

I let a sigh escape. I'm going to make sure *that* never happens again.

I examine the box from the library. The top flaps are folded into each other, but they're not sealed shut. I start to open it, but it occurs to me that mice might have climbed up into the box.

Can mice climb boxes? I don't think so. But just in case I missed something vital about the little brown mouse in my vast educational experience, I decide not to tempt fate. I pick up the box again and start to put it where I'd found it. Something shadowy on the wall behind where the box had been stacked catches my attention. I put the box down and hold up the lighter to see what it is. I laugh.

It's a lightbulb screwed into a fixture on the wall.

That means there's an electrical switch somewhere that will flood this tunnel with light. Now all I have to do is find the switch.

There should be one near the door to the game room and another one near the other, larger door, wherever that is.

"Boot!" I call out loudly.

He doesn't answer.

I keep moving along through the tunnel, past boxes, past a stack of wooden boards, past old cleaning tools like mops and brooms. Why didn't they just get rid of all this stuff?

I come to a wall in front of me; the tunnel makes a left-hand turn.

I follow it and see Boot off in the distance. He's stopped, and he's moving his light over the walls.

I make my way down to him.

"Hey, Boot—"

He looks up. "There's electricity in the tunnel," he says. He shines his light on another lightbulb.

"I know," I said. "Let's get to the big door, and I bet we'll find the light switch. Hold your light so it shines deeper."

He shines the penlight ahead of him. There's no end in sight.

He sneezes.

"You sure you want to be down here?" I say. "It's pretty cold."

He rolls his eyes. "You're just scared."

"That's not it," I say, halfway meaning it. "If you have a cold, it doesn't make sense for you to freeze yourself down here."

He scowls. "I'm okay, *Mom*."

"Coming to school with wet hair doesn't help, either. How come you don't dry it before you leave home?"

He shrugs. "I don't have time. I oversleep."

"So wake up earlier."

"I don't hear the alarm," he says. He looks away, then

back. "My dad wakes me up with water."

"He dumps water on you?"

He looks stricken, and I realize I just stepped over the line. So I shrug and say, "Hey, my dad wakes me up in the middle of the night for push-ups."

He doesn't respond.

"Come on, let's see where this tunnel ends," I tell him.

He nods and shines his light into the darkness, and I follow as he moves forward.

"I wonder if Mr. Maddox has discovered us gone with the tunnel door open," I say.

"He would have come down to get us," Boot replies.

"Yeah, you're probably right."

Boot stops and turns. "How much would a ticket to a Springsteen concert cost?"

"I don't know. Go online or call Ticketmaster."

"Yeah."

He turns away, and we start moving again.

"You practice a lot?" I ask.

"What do you mean?"

"You said you want to be in a band. Do you practice the guitar a lot?"

He shrugs. "Sometimes."

"Sometimes? How will you get to be in a band, if you only practice sporadically?"

"Why don't you just shut up?" He sounds mad.

"Okay. But if you want to get really good at something, you won't get there by just daydreaming about it."

"Mick—"

"Yeah?"

"Stuff it."

"Oh." I shrug. "Okay."

I switch the lighter to the other hand, but I'm careful to keep it lit the whole time, so I don't have to spin the hot wheel again. It's nearly a minute before he cries out, "There it is!"

I look where he's shining the light.

A set of seven steep stairs leads up to a landing and—*the big door.*

"Let's open it and see where it goes," I say.

He turns back to me, sort of smiling. "What if it's the girls' locker room?"

"Then we *gotta* try it," I tell him.

"Yeah."

We climb the stairs.

"Okay," I say, softening my voice, "turn off your light."

He does, and I let go of the lighter button.

It's so dark, I can't see *anything.*

"Let's take it slow and easy," I whisper. "I'll open it about an inch. Don't make a sound. We'll see what's there, and then I'll try to close it again without being seen."

"Okay."

"Ready?"

"Do it," he whispers.

I grasp the metal doorknob and turn it.

CHAPTER TWENTY-THREE

Boot's Turn

I SCRUNCH IN CLOSE, and Mick gives the door a very slow, quiet push.

It moves forward a little. The other side of the door has more light than the tunnel, but it's not bright.

I don't recognize it at first. But then the smell of soap and dust and cleaning chemicals hits my nose.

"We're inside the custodian's office," Mick whispers. He opens the door a little wider. "Nobody's here."

"Cool," I say. "We're on the other side of the building. There's the door that goes outside to the loading dock."

"Let's find the switch," Mick says, turning back into the tunnel.

We look near the door, but we don't see a switch. Then Mick looks on the wall inside the custodian's office, reaches in, and the tunnel floods with yellow light.

Mick's head jerks around, and he shoves me inside. He closes the door shut quiet behind him and puts a finger to his lips. I frown.

He points to the door and nudges me to go down the stairs to the floor of the tunnel. When we're at the bottom, he pulls me so my ear is close, and he whispers, "Get back to the game room quick."

We hurry back the way we came, this time with everything lit up bright around us.

Mick must have heard someone coming. Will the custodian notice that the light switch in her office is on? If so, she'll be sure to run this way to see who's down here.

We get to the ladder below the game-room door. I climb up first, and Mick scrambles up behind me. We're through the door before I remember to look for the light switch at this end. But Mick finds it. It's high up on the game-room wall. Some bookshelves are built around it, so you have to look to find it.

Mick snaps it off, and we close the tunnel door. I slide the desk back in front of it.

Mr. Maddox's voice comes from the doorway. "How was the checkers game?" he asks.

Mick's head whips around to face the doorway, and his body suddenly slouches to look very relaxed. "Great," he says. "Boot beat me over and over."

He laughs. "That right? Well, Boot, why don't you bring

your guitar tomorrow. I'd like to hear you play."

"Uh, sure," I say.

He leaves.

"He didn't ask why we're not at the coffee table," I say.

"I don't think he knows we were gone, though," Mick says. He's smiling.

"That was cool," I say. "Did you hear someone coming?"

"Yeah." He laughs. "I heard the custodian talking in the hallway. I think she was about to come into her office." His smile fades away. "Have you always had trouble hearing?"

"Just for a few years."

"What happened?"

"I—I don't know." I don't know what to say. "You ask too many questions."

He stares at me for a few seconds. Then he nods. "See ya."

"Yeah."

All afternoon I'm thinking about the Springsteen concert. Jesse would kill to see The Boss live in concert. If I could get him a ticket, I don't think he'd hate me so much.

My problem is that I don't have much money. Just ten dollars that Dad gave me for my birthday last month.

I'm getting a headache from my cold, and I feel pretty rotten. I just want to get out of school and go home and figure out how I can get a concert ticket. Finally at three o'clock, the bell rings, and I race to get out of the building. I'm pushing through the big front door when I see Tabitha walking down the hall.

"Hey, Boot!" she calls out and waves.

I stop. "Hey, Tab."

She hurries over. "How's it goin'?"

"Fine," I say. I snuff up and wipe my finger under my nose.

"Are you and Mick getting along now or something?" She looks like she hopes I'll say no.

"Getting along? No way."

She laughs. "But you're not getting into fights."

"Yeah," I say. "Maybe we're growing out of that."

"Really?" She thinks about that. "Bizarre."

"Yeah."

Maybe we have some aspirin at home for my headache. I'll look for some when I get home.

"What are you writing about for your science report?" she asks.

Science report? I don't remember hearing about that. I guess I was thinking about something else when it was mentioned.

"Oh, I don't know," I say. "Hey, have you ever bought concert tickets online at Ticketmaster?"

"No," she says. "But my dad went to the Corner Market once and got tickets there. It's a Ticketmaster outlet."

"Really? That's great. I need to stop there then."

"What are you going to get tickets to?" She looks excited.

"I want to get a friend a ticket for Bruce Springsteen."

Her eyes get really bright. "Boy, are you generous! It's not for Mick, is it?"

"Are you kidding? No."

She laughs. "I didn't think so."

"Okay, well, see you tomorrow," I say.

"Right."

I want to run all the way to the Corner Market, but my head aches too much, so I don't.

I pull open the door and go up to one of the women at a cash register. She turns to look at me, and I see she's got a few dark hairs growing out of her chin that curl up on the ends.

"You got Ticketmaster here?" I ask. I try not to look at the chin hairs, but it's hard not to because they look so weird.

"Yeah." She nods toward a counter at the side. "Talk to Debbie in customer service."

I walk over to the customer service counter where a girl about Ethan's age is standing. "Can I get a ticket to Bruce Springsteen's concert in Chicago?"

She doesn't even look at me, but starts typing on a computer. "October sixteenth?"

"Yeah, I guess so." Then I remember. "I just want to know how much a ticket costs."

She continues to type and then waits. "Seventy-five dollars."

She might as well have punched me in the stomach. *"Seventy-five dollars?"*

"Yeah." She looks at me for the first time. I walk away.

When I come through the back door, I realize I don't remember leaving the store and walking home. But I *am* home, and Moose is jumping all over me. I let him out in the backyard and watch him from the kitchen window.

I only have ten dollars. How do I get sixty-five more?

I have to get that money somehow. It's the only way I can make it up to Jesse. He'll be so happy about going to see Springsteen, and he'll keep remembering that I was the person who got him the ticket.

I think Ethan probably has sixty-five dollars in the bank. Maybe he'd loan it to me.

I go to the phone and open the cupboard and see where Ethan wrote his work number on the inside of the cupboard door. I dial, and it's answered right away.

"Hi, can I talk to Ethan Quinn?"

The lady who answers puts me on hold. I wait a while, and then it hits me that I shouldn't have called him at work. He'll be in a better mood tonight after he eats.

His voice comes on. "Hello?" He sounds like he's in a bad mood. There's no way he'll loan me the money now.

I hang up.

I'm sweating and nervous. *Why did I call him at work? That was stupid.*

The phone rings, and I answer it.

"Boot?"

Ethan.

"Oh. Hi."

"Why'd you call and hang up?" He's really mad.

"Oh, uh, sorry." *How did he know it was me?* The garage must have Caller ID. "I—I didn't mean to hang up. Moose jumped up, and I caught him, but I fell back against the—"

"Whaddayou want?"

"Uh, I just wondered, if—if—"

"*What?*"

"Could I borrow some money?" I clear my throat. "From you?"

He doesn't say anything for a few seconds. When he finally talks, his voice is stiff. "You called me up at work to ask if I'll loan you *money?*"

"Oh. Sorry . . ."

"How much?"

"What?"

He talks louder. "How much money are you asking for?"

"Oh . . . well. Sixty-five dollars?"

"*Are you out of your mind?*" He's yelling now. He must have slammed the receiver against the wall or something because I hear *BAM, BAM, BAM* so loud, it hurts my ear, and I have to take the phone away.

"Sorry, Eth—"

But before I can finish, he hangs up on me.

I put down the phone. My headache is really bad now, so I take some aspirin. I let Moose back inside and go downstairs to my room. I put on headphones, turn on music, and lie back on the bed. Ethan will calm down by the time he gets home. At least, I hope so. Maybe he won't even say anything about it.

I turn on my side. *How can I get that money?*

I see my guitar case across the room, and I sit up. *I could sell my guitar.* That other music store sells used instruments. *Maybe they'd buy it from me.*

If I save up enough money, I could buy another one later.

I get up, turn off the CD, grab the guitar, and take the steps up two at a time. It'll take a couple dollars for bus fare to get to the music store. But I'll get money on the guitar, so I'll be able to take the bus back home and still get the ticket for Jesse.

It takes me forty-five minutes on the bus, not counting the ten-minute wait to transfer downtown. We stop at every other corner the whole way, but the bus finally pulls up right in front of the store. It's a big white building at the edge of town.

MURPHY'S MUSIC is painted in red over the front door. A sign in the window says, WE BUY AND SELL USED INSTRUMENTS.

I pull open the heavy front door, walk in, and go up to the counter. A guy with thick glasses is on the phone, and another guy is talking to a mother and her kid who's about eight years old.

The guy on the phone hangs up and turns to me. "Can I help you?" He glances at the guitar case in my hand.

I lift it up and set it on the counter. "I want to sell this guitar."

He opens the case and takes it out. He strums a few chords, and it's horribly out of tune. He makes a face.

I should've tuned it before I left home.

He takes a minute and tunes it. He strums. "Not bad," he says.

"Yeah," I say. "It's got a great sound."

He plays it some more.

"Okay," he says. He puts it down and takes out a piece of paper. He starts writing. "With the case, I'll give you forty-five for it," he says.

"*Forty-five dollars?*" I say. "It's worth a *lot* more than that."

He stops writing and looks at me. "That's my offer. You want it or not?"

"Sixty-five," I say.

"Forty-five," he says. "Take it or leave it." He looks away and jiggles the pen between his pointer and middle fingers, like he's really impatient.

"*Take it.*" It comes out mad, and I don't care. I'm still twenty-two dollars short. Twenty-four after I take the bus home.

He opens the register, gets the money, and counts it out on the counter. Then he picks up my guitar and walks away with it.

My guitar. As I stuff the cash into my pocket, I watch my guitar disappear with him into a room in the back. I had my guitar lessons on it. I was going to get real good on it; then I was going to buy myself an electric guitar.

I'll get the money somehow before too long and buy another one.

All the way home on the bus, I think about the twenty-four dollars that I need. I doubt if Dad would loan it to me. He'd want to know why I want the money, and I don't want to go into that part.

I get home about five-thirty, and I see Ethan's car in front. I hope he's not still mad. I peek in the window as I walk around to the back, and I see him sitting on the couch, eating. He must have stopped at Wendy's. A big Wendy's cup is on the coffee table.

I walk in the back door and hear MTV playing loud. I don't want to bother him, and I'm hungry, so I find a pot and start water boiling for mac and cheese.

I go into the living room and sit on the other end of the couch. I don't say anything, in case he's still mad.

"What do you need sixty-five dollars for?" he asks without taking his eyes off the TV.

"I just wanted to get a ticket for the Bruce Springsteen concert," I tell him.

He looks over at me. "Springsteen's not coming here."

"No," I say. "Chicago."

"And how do you think you'd get to Chicago?"

"I don't know."

He looks like he thinks I'm the stupidest person on earth. "You got any brains in that head?"

I don't answer.

He doesn't say anything more and goes back to eating and watching TV.

Dad comes home just when the mac and cheese is ready. By that time, Ethan is finished eating and has gone somewhere in his car. Dad switches to the news, and we sit on the couch and eat.

I can tell he had a bad day at work by the way he stabs at his food. So I don't say anything.

About halfway through eating, he says, "Get me a beer, will you?"

So I go to the fridge and look inside. The lightbulb's burned out, so I can't see too well in there. But I don't see any beer. I close the door and go back to the living room. "We don't have any."

Dad swears and shoves another forkful of mac and cheese into his mouth.

When we're done eating, I take both our plates into the kitchen, put them in the sink, and run water on them. I turn off the water and start to walk to the basement steps, but I see the sugar bowl on the counter.

I wonder how much money is in there. I wonder if there's more than twenty-four dollars—and if Dad would notice if that much was gone for a little while.

I can hear my heart *kathunk*ing in my ears. It's too risky to look now. Maybe I'll get a chance later.

I go downstairs and listen to music. I don't hear it, though. I'm picturing myself getting the money, buying the Springsteen ticket, and taking it to Jesse tomorrow. He'll be suspicious when he sees me. He might even tell me to leave. But then I'll pull out the ticket and hand it to him.

Thinking about that makes me smile, 'cause I know *he'll* be smiling. And he'll go to the concert, and when he gets home, he'll probably call me and tell me about seeing Springsteen live. And he'll thank me. I'll tell him again how sorry I am for taking that flute, and I'll tell him again that it was a dare, and I was a jerk for taking it. And he'll know I'm really sorry.

I take off the headphones. I don't hear the TV, so I walk

up the stairs. The TV is off, and Dad's not in the living room. I look out the window, and the car's gone from the garage. But he didn't leave me a note, so I figure he won't be gone long. He probably went to the HandiMart to get beer.

My hands are suddenly clammy, but I go get the sugar bowl and take it to the living room and dump out the money on the couch. I count out fifty-three dollars and ninety-four cents.

Way more than I need.

I could go to the Corner Market right now—they're open pretty late—get the ticket, and it could be in Jesse's hand by tomorrow after school. It's exciting to think I could make him happy in less than a day.

I take thirty dollars, so I'm sure to have enough for the tax, and stuff it in my pocket with the forty-five from Murphy's Music and the six dollars left from my birthday money.

I go out the back door and head for the Corner Market. It only takes about twenty minutes to walk there. I open the door and go right to customer service. It's a different lady working there. I tell her what I want and put the money on the counter.

She smiles while she counts it. "You must be a big Springsteen fan," she says.

I'm not going to tell her the whole story, so I say, "Yeah."

She asks if I want to sit on an aisle or in the middle of a

row. I tell her wherever is closest.

She gives me the ticket, and I slide it into my pocket. Seventy-five dollars' worth of ticket. It's hard to believe that little thing costs so much money.

I leave, and while I walk home, I try out a few ways to tell Jesse about it.

I got a surprise for you, Jesse. Something you really want.

Then I'll take it out of my pocket and hand it to him. *It's for you. I just wanted to give it to you. To say I'm sorry.*

But that sounds kind of sappy, and besides, he might try to throw me out of the store before I get it out of my pocket.

So I try it a different way. *Before you make me leave, I just want to give you something.* Then I'll hand it to him. *It's for you, Jess. So you can go to Chicago and see The Boss.*

That sounds okay. He'll frown at first till he sees that it really *is* a ticket to the concert. Then he'll have to smile.

I can't wait to give it to him.

When I get home, my dad's standing in the middle of the kitchen floor. He looks really mad.

"*Where's Ethan?*" he yells. I can smell beer on him, but I don't think he's drunk.

Then I see he's holding the sugar bowl. He's grabbing it so tight, his fingers are white.

I can hardly breathe. "Uh, I don't know."

"Did you see him take money out of the sugar bowl?"

"No." It comes out a whisper.

He slams it down on the counter, not hard enough to break it, but I hear some coins clinking inside.

"I took twenty dollars out to get some gas, but even after that, there was over fifty dollars in here." His face is red, and he's yelling. "Now there's thirty dollars gone. *Where's Ethan?*"

"I don't know," I say.

"If he took that money—" He stops and looks at me. I'm shaking all over, and I can't stop. "*You? You took my money?*"

He takes a step toward me, and I take a step back. Then he backhands me so hard, I lose my balance and land on the floor.

"*You steal from your own father?*" he yells at me. "*You're good for nothing, just like your brother.*"

I put my hand to my mouth, and when I pull it back, I see it's bloody.

Dad grabs me by my shirt and hauls me off the floor. "*Where is it?*" he screams. "*What did you do with my money? Hunh? Where is it, you little thief?*"

He shakes me till my teeth chatter, then shoves me into the kitchen cabinet. I fall on the floor. I know what's coming, so I curl up in a tight ball, and he kicks my back, my arms, and my leg. I keep myself from crying, and maybe that makes him madder. He punches with one fist and the other, screaming the whole time, "*Where is it? Where's my money?*"

Then I do something I've never done before. I grab his foot and yank hard enough to make him lose his balance and fall. I get up fast, pull the ticket out of my pocket, and throw it at him.

"There it is, you bastard," I yell at him. *"Go get your money back. I hate you. I HATE you."*

I pull open the kitchen door that's right behind me, and I run outside, and around the house. And I run, and run, and run.

CHAPTER TWENTY-FOUR

Mick's Turn

I'M READING IN bed before going to sleep, and Dad stops in the doorway. The packing boxes that Mom got for me are sitting in front of my closet.

"So you're moving out, too?" he says.

"Yeah." I close the book and sit up. We have to have this conversation; I can't avoid it any longer.

He comes into my room and sits on the edge of my bed.

"Mick," he says, "I promise you I'll never take another drink if you'll stay."

This sounds suspiciously like blackmail.

So I say, "And if I don't stay, and you take a drink, it'll be my fault?"

Let's call a spade a spade.

"No, it's not that," he says. "But I won't have the incentive if you're gone. It's going to be so lonely around here."

I remember the Alcoholic game. I'm not playing.

"I know," I say. "Mom's been lonely a lot when you didn't come home for days at a time. She doesn't deserve for me to abandon her."

"I know. You're right," he says. "And I *do* deserve it."

I'm not playing. I fold my arms over my chest and say nothing.

He looks around the room at my computer on the desk, my tall bookshelf holding books by my favorite writers: Flannery O'Connor, John Irving, Dean Koontz, Richard Matheson, Stephen King. "You were only three when we moved into this house. I've always been sentimental about this room—because it's yours." He sighs heavily. "It just won't be the same."

I'm not playing.

He leans forward, his back hunched, and puts his head in his hands. "I'm just so sorry, Mick. I've been a terrible dad to you."

I can't stand not saying anything. "Only when you're drinking," I tell him softly.

He looks up. "I was doing okay this time," he says. His voice takes on an edge. "Until Dave called."

I don't blink. "This isn't your brother's fault."

"I know," he says, putting up his hands. "It's *my* fault. But he comes here acting so—holier than thou. He stopped drinking and joined AA, so he thinks he's better than me. He threw it in my face, how great he's doing in his business, how beautiful his wife is, how *perfect* everything in his life is. I know he thinks I'm a bum."

I stay quiet.

He straightens up. "So this is it," he says. "You're moving out."

"Mom and I'll see you when you're sober," I remind him. "And you'll be busy; you have to find a new job."

"Will you help me mow the lawn?" he asks.

I'm not sure how to answer. "I don't know," I say. "I'll probably need to get a job mowing and shoveling snow to help pay for the apartment."

"That's why this doesn't make *sense*," he says. "*You* shouldn't have to support your mother. That's *my* job."

I don't remind him that he currently doesn't have a job. Or that we've always lived on Mom's paycheck when he drank his.

"Mom and I'll be okay," I say. "Mom's amazing at making a dollar stretch."

"She sure is."

I see tears in his eyes again, and I feel myself weakening. I look away.

I'm not playing.

"Sorry, Dad, but I've got to get up for school tomorrow, so I need to get some sleep."

I turn back. He nods, blinking tears onto his cheeks, and gets up.

"Well, if you have to leave, I guess you have to leave."

I extend my hand, and he takes it. "'Night, Dad," I say.

He nods, drops my hand, and walks out of my room. He leaves the door open, and I hear him crying as he walks down the hall and into the living room.

I quietly get up and close the door, so I don't hear him. I get into bed and turn out the lamp on my bedside table.

I lie there awake in the dark for more than two hours before I finally fall asleep.

The morning at school feels long and boring. I'm tired because, even after I finally got to sleep last night, I didn't sleep very well. I try to keep the image of my dad with his head in his hands out of my mind. I didn't realize how good alcoholics and their families are at playing their games until I read the library book that Laura gave me.

I hope if Mom and I stop playing, Dad will stop, too. And maybe he'll stop drinking and get his life straightened out. He's the only person who can do it.

At eleven o'clock, I go to the principal's office and wait for Boot. I sit there and watch Mrs. Taylor while she fiddles with the shade on the window. It's pulled all the way down, and she keeps yanking on it, trying to get it to slide up. I watch her; she's amazingly tenacious, but she gets more and more frustrated as it becomes clear that the shade isn't going to move. When I was in elementary school, we had a bulldog named Brutus, and Mom gave him an old tennis shoe to play with. He'd grab it in his teeth and shake it violently as if he was trying to kill it. Mrs. Taylor reminds me of Brutus; I think she's trying to teach that window shade a lesson about behaving.

Five minutes later, Mr. Maddox comes out. "Boot's not here yet?"

"No," I say.

He picks up the phone and calls the attendance office. "Hi, this is Pete Maddox," he says. "Is Boot Quinn absent today?" He listens for a few seconds. "Okay. Thanks."

He puts down the phone. "No game room today, Mick. Boot's absent."

"Okay."

I would never have believed it a week ago, but I'm kind of disappointed. Ol' Boot can actually be entertaining when he wants to be. And besides, I'd rather think about playing a game or exploring the tunnel than thinking about my dad.

I guess the cold Boot had yesterday finally kicked his feet out from under him.

"Good luck with that shade, Mrs. Taylor," I call out

to her. She's still yanking and doesn't bother to acknowledge me.

I go back to class.

At lunchtime, I go to the caf and pick up my food. I walk to my old table near the wall and sit down with Adam and Connor. They look over at me, surprised.

"You don't have to go to the game room anymore?" Adam asks.

"Boot's sick," I say.

"How long is your game-room sentence, anyway?" Connor asks.

"I don't know. I guess until we can stand each other."

Adam laughed. "And that'll be . . . never?"

I shrug. I haven't really thought about it seriously, but Boot and I do seem to have called a truce. Making him miserable has lost its fun; maybe the dares took the fun out of it. And with all that's going on at home, I'm just not in the mood. I think maybe he doesn't hate me as much anymore, either.

"I guess we've called some sort of truce," I tell them.

They go back to their eating and the conversation that I interrupted.

I take a bite of the hamburger on my plate, and while I'm chewing, Tabitha appears. She's smiling, as she hurries up to the table.

"Aren't you guys in the game room anymore?" she asks.

"Boot's sick," I tell her.

"Oh. Yeah, he seemed to have a cold yesterday."

Adam speaks up. "Put any slash marks on the locker room wall lately?"

Tabitha opens her mouth, but nothing comes out. In about five seconds, her blush turns her face nearly crimson.

"Did you guys hear about that?" she asks in a little voice. She's looking at me.

"Who finally won?" I ask.

"It's a tie," she says. She tips her head to one side. "So you have any more fights coming up?"

"I don't know," I say. "I guess you'll have to be surprised."

She laughs. "Let me know if anything's brewing."

"Sure," I tell her. "You'll be the first to know."

She laughs again and hurries off.

I turn to Adam and Connor. "Maybe Boot and I should stage a fight. I could be magnanimous and let him win." I wonder if I could really do that with everybody standing around watching. Probably not.

Adam rolls his eyes and goes back to his conversation with Connor.

I don't want to go home after school. It's hard to be stoic while Dad tries to make me feel guilty for moving, so I head for the library. I don't want to see the empty spot where the statue was, and I get an unpleasant feeling in my stomach as I get close.

But when I come around the corner and the library's in view, I see that the boy and his grandmother are back. And all the paint is gone.

I can feel the tightness in my stomach loosening. I pull in a breath and let it go. The statue looks beautiful.

Inside, I see Laura at the circulation desk. She's talking to a girl, and I would have to be blind not to notice that this girl is hot.

"Hey," I say.

Laura smiles. "Hey, yourself, Mick. Say hello to my sister, Jane. Jane, this is Mick Sullivan."

Jane turns to me and smiles. She's a little younger than Laura—probably about my age.

"Hi," I say. I'm glad Laura didn't request that I say anything more than hello, because—in front of the second girl in the last couple of weeks—I'm tongue-tied. And on top of that, thirty-four new jets of various sizes appear out of nowhere and zoom down the runway in my chest.

"Hi," she says. Her smile is exactly like Laura's. The sky is now decorated with soaring and zooming aircraft.

"Jane just started volunteering. She wants to be able to get a job here when she turns sixteen."

"Great," I manage to say. "You . . . like to read?"

Please say yes.

The brightness in her eyes intensifies. "It's my passion," she says.

If I died suddenly, and this is heaven, please don't resuscitate.

She's leaning forward over the circulation desk, smiling and staring into my eyes. So I've got to go out on a limb here and say she looks interested in me, too. *Man, I hope I'm right.*

"She had a good interview, so they accepted her," Laura says. She's grinning and I see that her glance is bouncing back and forth between Jane and me.

Then it hits me: Jane will be here *regularly.*

Is this my lucky day or what?

Laura's looking over my shoulder. "There's Ms. Bracton, Jane. Let's get to work."

Jane smiles at me. "Nice to meet you," she says, and they move off.

I'm not sure, but I think my body defies the laws of physics and floats home in the afternoon sunshine.

Dad isn't home when I get there. I go to my room and do homework for an hour.

Mom gets home and stops on her way down the hall.

"Hi, honey." She leans against the doorway.

"Hey."

"Isn't your dad home?"

"No, I haven't seen him."

She frowns. "Okay. I'll get going on supper."

"What are we having?"

"Stir-fry. I want to get rid of some fresh and frozen vegetables. Your dad won't fix them for himself."

"Okay." She disappears.

Dad still isn't home when Mom calls me to eat. We sit at the dining room table.

"We can move into the apartment a week from this weekend," Mom says. "Okay with you? We should be able to do it ourselves. Joanie at work said we could use her dolly for the heavy stuff."

"Okay," I say. "What furniture are we taking?"

"The couch, your bed and desk, half the dishes, all our clothes."

"TV?"

"I think we should leave that for your dad," she says.

"Okay." Dad's the TV watcher in the family. I can read the news online.

When the phone rings, Mom jumps up. I know she's hoping it's Dad.

"Hello?" Disappointment passes over her face. "Yes, he's here."

I get up and take the phone from her.

"Mick?"

Female. Jane?

"It's me, Tabitha."

"Hey," I say.

Okay, so I had a spasm of unrealistic hope. Deal with it.

"I just called Boot to see how he's doing?"

"Yeah?"

"His dad says he's run away!"

"Run *away*? Did he say why?"

"No," she says. "He just said he ran off last night and hasn't come back. He asked me if I knew where he was."

"I just thought he was sick today."

"Yeah, me, too. I wonder what happened? Well, if you hear anything, will you tell him to give me a call?"

"Sure."

We say good-bye and hang up. I sit at the table again.

"Who's run away?" Mom asks.

"Boot."

"Were things going poorly at school?" she asks. "Are you guys still playing games?"

"Yes, but when he didn't show up, I thought he was sick . . ."

And then I realize where Boot is. Maybe it's the only secret place he knows.

"Uh, Mom? I think I know where he might be. You mind if I . . ."

"No, go ahead. I hope you find him."

I get up and walk straight out the back door. Striding across the back patio, I look at my watch; it's nearly six-thirty.

When I get to school, I try the front door. It's locked. I wander around the building, looking for lights on in classrooms. If Greg, the night custodian, is in a room on the ground floor, I can wave at him from the window and ask him to let me in. He's not all that friendly, but he's not mean. I think he'd let me.

Wait. That's a bad idea. If Greg lets me in, he'll want to know why I'm here. And he'll follow me to find out what I'm going to do. I want to see Boot alone.

So how am I going to get inside?

I circle around to the back and see the football team practicing on the field. Maybe the gym door is open.

I jog to the gym door and pull. It opens, and I walk inside. The custodian's office is on the far side of the school, so I decide to get into the tunnel from the game room. Besides, Greg is less likely to see me there.

I hurry through the locker room and into the hall. I run to the end of the hall, but before turning the corner, I peek around it to make sure nobody's there. I don't see anyone, so I run the rest of the way.

I stop in front of the principal's office and walk through the door.

Greg is standing at the window. His back is to me while

he shakes the shade that Mrs. Taylor was fighting this morning. I duck down in front of the counter, so he can't see me.

I hear flapping as he shakes the shade. I crawl to the end of the counter and peek over the top. Greg uses a chair to step up onto the radiator. He reaches up and takes the shade off its support on the window frame and rolls it up. Then he puts it back. He tests it a few times, pulling it down partway and snapping it back up.

The shade works again. So he jumps down to the floor, crosses the office, and strides out the door into the hall.

I wait a few seconds in case he forgot something, but he doesn't return, so, still hunched down, I run across the office and into the game room.

The desk is pulled back from the wall, but not far. Boot would've had to pull the desk back in toward the wall with his arm snaking around the edge of the tunnel door.

I push the desk back farther, squat down, and open the door.

If Boot is down here, he's waiting in the dark. The lights are off.

I stand up to flip the light switch but stop. If I turn on the lights, he won't know it's me, and he'll think the custodian's coming. He'll run.

But I forgot to bring a flashlight.

But I don't want to go down there in the dark.

Okay, so my choices are: 1) go home and get the flashlight

and risk getting caught trying to get inside again, or 2) go down into the tunnel in the dark. I have to decide. Which is the stronger flaw in my personality: laziness or fear?

That's a hard one.

Okay, laziness.

I swing my legs through the door and onto the ladder.

Oh, man. If there are mice down here, I don't have a light to scare them away. And it's pitch-dark.

"Boot?" I call out. Maybe he has a flashlight and will turn it on.

No answer. He might not even be here.

Or maybe he doesn't hear me.

I *really* don't want to go deeper into the tunnel. "Boot?" Still no answer.

I listen for little mice feet, but it's all quiet.

I close the tunnel door behind me, and it's totally black. I hold my breath and wait for my eyes to adjust to the dark, but it doesn't get any better. Even after about half a minute, I can't see anything. I wave my hand in front of my face. Nothing.

I push the door open again. At least this way I can see a few feet into the tunnel. There's no sign of Boot.

I climb down the ladder one rung at a time, listening for mice. At the bottom, I call out, "Boot?" again. No response.

Go on, get it over with. I take eight or nine steps till I get to the point where the shadows abruptly get deeper and the light from the tunnel door ends.

Ahead of me looms total darkness.

I take another step and reach out. A box corner stands to the side, so keeping a hand on the box, I walk around it.

"Boot?"

I take another step, and another, very slowly, inching my way deeper into the blackness.

Man, I was stupid not to think to bring a flashlight.

"Boot?"

I take baby steps, one by one, not wanting to go forward, but forcing myself. I get slower and slower. In two minutes, I've probably only gone about fifteen feet. I can remember where a lot of the stuff is down here, and most of what I touch is familiar.

It probably takes ten minutes for me to get down to the elbow of the tunnel. The boxes and stuff turn me to the left. I'm now close to where I found Boot the last time we were down here.

Something scuttles over my foot, and I scream, *"MICE!"*

I whirl around in the darkness, my heart fluttering hysterically, and I scramble back the same way I came, back toward the game room.

"Mick."

I think I hear it, and I stop. I'm breathing so hard, I'm not sure if it was real or I imagined it.

"Boot?"

"Over here," he says.

"*Boot?* Come on, let's get out of here. There're mice in this tunnel!" I say.

"Duh."

"*Come on!*"

He doesn't answer, but I'm so jumpy, I'm hopping up and down. *I like mice. I love mice. I wish I had mice in my room at home.*

Okay, okay. *Get hold of yourself.* I make myself relax. I force myself to take deep breaths.

"I guess . . ." My voice is shaking, so I take another breath. "I guess I can stand the mice if you can," I say finally.

"Yeah, right."

Wise guy.

I inch toward his voice. "Are you okay?" I ask.

"Depends on what you mean," he says. "At least I'm not afraid of mice."

Smart guy.

"Where are you?" I ask.

"You can't see any landmarks," he says. "So you better just follow my voice. No, wait."

A flame bursts alive just ahead of me. He's wrapped himself up in a dirty old packing blanket. He's sitting on a box and holding the lighter just in front of his chin.

"Man," I say, focused on his face. "*What happened to you?*"

His face is mottled with bruises, and dried blood is caked on his shirt.

"Who beat you up?"

He opens his mouth, then closes it and shakes his head.

"Your dad." I don't ask it; I already know. "Why?"

Before he looks down, I see the water in his eyes. "I stole his money." He's hunched over, hugging one arm to his chest.

"Geez, how much did you take?"

He says it quietly. "Thirty dollars."

I gawk at him. "Your dad beat you up over *thirty stinking dollars?*"

He lets the lighter flame go out. I hear him sniff; he's crying.

"I wanted to get Jesse a concert ticket, so he wouldn't hate me."

"So he wouldn't hate you for shoplifting?"

"Yeah."

Oh, man. My throat is suddenly dry.

"I'm sorry, Boot," I tell him. "Are you okay?"

He's crying as softly as possible, but a little sob escapes. I reach out and touch his arm. He leans in and rests his forehead against my shoulder. I can feel him trembling.

I pat him awkwardly on the arm, and he cries out.

"What?" I ask, jumping back.

He breathes heavily. "I think it's broken."

"What's broken?" I ask him.

"My arm."

"He broke your arm, too?"

"He didn't mean to."

That may be the most pathetic thing I've ever heard anyone say. "We've got to get you to a doctor," I tell him.

"No. No doctor."

"Are you nuts?"

"No doctor." He sounds scared.

"Boot, you can't stay down here forever."

"If I go to a doctor, they'll put me in a foster home."

"Has someone tried to do that before?" I ask.

"No, but I heard about another guy."

"That's why you don't hear well, right? One too many punches in the head."

His voice comes out in gasps as he tries to stop crying. "I don't know why he doesn't like me."

How do I respond to that?

"Your dad likes you," I say, but how do I know? Because every father *should* like his kid? How can a father who loves his son beat him up?

My dad has gotten physical—shoved Mom and me around—but he's never beaten us up. I know, I know. Shoving us around is bad enough. But it's a matter of degree somehow. Sort of. More or less.

Okay, less.

But I can't get around the fact that—

"Mick." It's a whisper.

"What?"

"Do you have anything to eat?"

He hasn't eaten since yesterday.

I pull a half-eaten roll of Life Savers from my pocket. "Give me your hand." I fumble for his hand, put the candy on his palm, and curl his fingers around them.

In a few seconds, I hear him tearing off the wrapper and crunching as he devours them.

"I don't know what to do," he says finally.

"Are you afraid your dad will beat you again?"

He doesn't answer; he's making little noises, still crying.

And I'm suddenly really mad.

"Okay, Boot," I say. "I won't make you go to a doctor. But I'm going to do *something*."

"What?" he asks in a small voice.

"Never mind."

"What?" he asks again, louder this time.

But I've already started back the way I came. I'm faster this time, though. I don't care that it's dark. I don't care that there are mice in the tunnel. I don't care about anything—

I'm going to have my say.

It might seem strange that I can forgive my own dad for getting drunk and shoving my mom, but I'm in a blind rage about

Boot's dad who takes it a step further and beats him up. Boot's dad is a jerk, and I hate him for what he's done to his kid.

Boot's calling me as I climb the ladder, but I pretend I don't hear. I scramble through the door, stride across the game room, through the principal's office, down the hall, and out the front door into the cool evening.

I don't slow down until I get to Boot's house. I haven't seen it since I decorated the trees around it with toilet paper in sixth grade. I can feel my legs get a tiny bit weak as I walk up to the door, but I'm still really mad, and I bang the door knocker against its brass base.

The door is yanked open and a guy—not Boot's dad—stands there. He's older than I am, probably Boot's brother.

"Your dad here?" I say. It comes out loud.

The guy's eyes go to slits, like he thinks I'm challenging him, and he doesn't want to look weak. Geez, I see where Boot got his stupid macho act. The guy takes in my size, though, and I'm a little taller than he is, and I've probably got at least fifteen pounds on him.

"Who is it?" The voice comes from behind him, and Boot's dad steps into the doorway.

He looks me over with one glance. "What is it?"

"It's Boot," I tell him.

"Where is he?" His voice is sharp, and I can't tell if he's mad at Boot or at me for having the nerve to knock on his door.

"Don't you mean, '*How* is he?'" I say. "I'll tell you how he is, Mr. Quinn. He's got bruises all over his face, blood on his shirt, and maybe a broken arm."

Quinn's eyes go narrow like his older son, and anger flashes in his eyes. He steps toward me, holding an index finger near my nose. "You tell me where he is."

"*Or what?*" I say. I swell up to my full height, a little taller than he is. "You gonna give *me* a black eye? Or make *me* deaf in one ear?"

Quinn flinches at that like he's surprised. *He didn't know?*

"Or break my arm? *You gonna treat me like you treat your own flesh and blood, Mr. Quinn?*"

The brother steps in front of him and gives me a hard shove. I stumble backward, and Mr. Quinn grabs his son from behind.

"Stop it," he says. He moves Boot's brother to one side, and he lowers his voice. "Take me to him."

"Why should I?" I say. "You gonna beat him up again?"

He stands there and stares at me for a long time. Then he lowers his eyes. "No. I'm not going to hurt him."

I'm not sure why, but I believe him.

"I'll show you," I say.

"I'll get the car."

Boot's brother stands next to the driveway and watches me climb into the car and close the door. I look at Boot's dad who gives me a nod and backs into the street.

"This way," I say, pointing. The car reeks of cigarettes, which reminds me. "Do you have a lighter?"

He glances at me and back to the road. Then he reaches into his pocket, pulls one out, and hands it to me.

When I take it and don't light a cigarette, he looks over at me again. I say, "We'll need it at school."

"That's where we're going?"

"Yes."

We don't say anything more. I sneak a peek at him when we round a corner, but I can't read his face. He doesn't seem too angry now, but his face has a hard look, like he's posing for the making of a bronze statue of himself.

What's he thinking? Am I doing the right thing, taking him to Boot?

It's not too late to change my mind. But so far, Quinn isn't acting crazy. If he really does try to hurt Boot, though, I'm pretty sure I can take him. I'm not a lot bigger than he is, but I'm a little bigger.

"Park near the gym," I say, and he pulls into a spot at the far corner of the parking lot.

We get out of the car, and he follows me through the gym door. The guys have finished football practice and are milling around in front of the locker room. Some of them turn to look at us, but no one says anything.

I lead Mr. Quinn down the hall and around the corner

to the principal's office, then into the game room. The desk is still standing away from the wall. I lean down and open the tunnel door.

"Follow me," I say.

I sit down in the doorway and slide onto the ladder.

"Come on," I say. "He's down here."

Mr. Quinn hesitates a second, then follows me into the tunnel.

CHAPTER TWENTY-FIVE

Boot's Turn

A LONG WAY DOWN the tunnel, I see a flame bouncing in the blackness as Mick walks toward me.

Where did he go? Where did he get a lighter?

I almost climbed out of the tunnel after he left. I wanted to. The pain in my arm is the worst thing, but I'm still real hungry and even with the blanket, it's really cold down here. But I didn't know where to go.

I didn't know where Mick was going, but I knew I could trust him not to tell anyone where I am. I think I learned that much about him. I squint at the flame getting close, and my heart nearly stops. Behind the flame is Mick, but behind Mick is someone else.

He told.

I can't see who it is, and I freeze. There's no way I can

get out of here before they reach me.

In seconds, they stop in front of me. Mick moves to the side, and I see him.

I can't stop the rush of air that escapes from my lungs. Before I can say anything, Mick says, "Here he is, Mr. Quinn. You really messed him up good this time. Boot, show him your bruises, and all the blood. Tell your old man how he broke your arm, and how his beatings have made you nearly deaf in one ear."

Mick's really mad, and I watch my dad's face. I'm scared he's going to start a fight with Mick or me, but he doesn't. He just stares at me.

Mick turns back to Dad. "One thing I didn't tell you, Mr. Quinn, is that Boot took your money because of something I dared him to do. He didn't take the money for himself. He needed it for a friend, to make things right."

He waits to see what my dad does next. Dad turns to him and says, "I want to talk to my son."

"I don't know . . ." Mick says.

"I told you I won't hurt him," Dad says.

Mick seems to study Dad's face. Then he says to me, "I'll wait for you back at the ladder, Boot. Call me if you need anything."

He moves past my dad, taking the lighter with him. I pull my lighter out of my pocket and flick it on.

My dad clears his throat and shifts his weight over the

other foot. I wait for him to say something.

"Boot, you come on home with me now."

I'm scared, but I look at him straight on. "I'm not going back home with you," I tell him. "I don't want to get hit anymore. I'd rather stay here."

My dad frowns and stares at me. "What's he mean about a dare?"

"We were playing a dare game," I say. "Mick dared me to steal something from River City Music." He doesn't say anything, so I go on. "I got caught and Jesse and his dad at the store told me to never come back. I wanted to get Jesse a concert ticket to try to make it up to him."

Dad doesn't say anything for a long time.

Finally, he says, "I want you to come home now."

"I'm not going," I say.

My dad scratches his head and his eyes shift from me to the floor and back up to me again.

"When I was a boy, my dad used to get mad and knock me around. I hated my dad, and I swore I'd never do it to my kid." He stares at the floor again, and a long time goes by. Then he says, "I won't hit you."

His voice is soft, and I want to think he means it, but I don't know.

"Come on, Boot," he says. "Let's go home."

I look at his face. He doesn't look mad. I really do want to go home. At least there's food at home, and it's not freezing.

I slide off the box. "I need to get my arm checked first," I tell him. "In case I broke it. It really hurts."

He nods. Then he turns around and walks ahead of me through the tunnel.

Mick is waiting at the bottom of the ladder. When he sees us, he shuts off his lighter and climbs up in front of us.

I take hold of the ladder, but pain rips through me when I try to pull myself up with my arm. I can't stop the sound that comes out of my mouth.

"Put your arm around my neck," Dad says. "Lean on me."

I put my other arm around his neck, and we climb the ladder. Mick helps me get through the tunnel door.

Inside the game room, we shut the tunnel door and push the desk in front of it.

Dad looks at Mick for a second. Then he nods at him and walks across the floor and out of the game-room door.

I look at Mick. "You want a ride home?"

"No," he says. "I think I'll just walk."

"Okay." I'm kind of glad. I'd rather not have Mick in the car right now, and besides, the hospital is the other way.

Mick and I walk through the principal's office and out into the hall. Dad is nearly to the front door now, but Mick and I stop here, back a ways.

"See you tomorrow at school," he says.

"Okay."

"You can call me if you need to, you know," he says.

"I know," I tell him.

He stares off at my dad. Then he nods at me and strolls away down the hall.

CHAPTER TWENTY-SIX

Mick's Turn

WHEN I WAKE UP the next morning, Dad still isn't home. All Mom says is, "His life is in his hands."

I guess that says it all. She's reserved a trailer to move our stuff a week from Saturday. She's also starting some legal procedures, so if Dad doesn't pay the mortgage and his bills, her own finances won't be ruined.

She seems—I don't know—*lighter* since deciding to leave. I guess she took the load she'd been carrying for fourteen years called "Dad's welfare" off her shoulders and gave it back to him. She's laughing more and listening more intently when I talk.

I still worry about Dad. I hope he can figure out how to dry out and stay that way, and how to take care of himself. That's a lot for anyone to learn all at once.

* * *

When I get to school, I look for Boot, but I don't see him. After first period, I see Tabitha and Cheyanne in the hall and wave to them. They hurry over.

"Did you and Boot get in a fight again?" Tabitha asks. "I hear he's got bruises and an arm in a cast! I've been looking all over for him."

"No, I haven't seen him."

"So did you guys fight?"

This time she's frowning. She must have realized that Boot's injuries were pretty serious. I say, "Nope, I'm not responsible for that."

Then I see him rounding the corner and loping toward us. Tabitha runs over to him, takes hold of his hand, and walks him back to us.

"How did you get hurt, Boot?" she asks. "Mick swears it's not his fault."

He sees me and smiles at her. "Oh, I just tripped over my dog and fell down the basement stairs at home."

He glances at me again, but looks away.

I laugh. "What an oaf."

I see a flash of gratitude in his eyes just before he catches himself. "Yeah, well, if you want to try it," he says, "I'll go to any stairs you choose and give you a shove."

Tabitha and Cheyanne laugh. "You guys!" Tabitha says, tipping her head to the side. She's still holding his hand.

And I don't feel anything.

It's pretty nice not to be hung up on her anymore. Very liberating.

I don't see Boot again until eleven o'clock. I get to the principal's office, and he's already there. I collapse into the chair next to him.

"How's the arm?" I ask.

"Okay." He holds up his cast. "I've got to wear this for six weeks."

"And no one's signed it yet?"

He shrugs. "No, I didn't think about it."

I stand up. "Mrs. Taylor, do you have a marker?"

She looks suspicious, so I say, "I'm not going to commit vandalism. I'm signing Boot's cast."

She doesn't look convinced, but she opens her drawer. "Black or red?"

"Red."

I take the marker she hands me and walk back to Boot and sit again. I take off the marker's top and write:

> *Boot doesn't like math or work or books,*
> *But he's not as stupid as he looks.*
> *—Mick*

"Not bad for an instant rhyme," I say.

He rolls his eyes but smiles. "Thanks. For . . ." He shrugs. "You know."

"Yeah." I give the marker back to Mrs. Taylor who looks relieved that she doesn't have to call the custodian to scrub marks off the walls. I sit down again. "What happened when you got home?"

"He gave me back the concert ticket, but I have to work off the thirty dollars."

"That's great."

"Yeah," he says. "I'm going to take it to Jesse after school." He shrugs again. "Dad's got a temper, that's all. Sometimes he just can't control himself."

No kidding. "Yeah," I say.

"I told him if he hits me again, I'm going to go and live with my aunt Sarah."

"So maybe he won't hit you again," I say. That's probably not likely, but at least he has a plan.

Mr. Maddox steps out of his office and waves at us to come back. We get up and walk around the office counter.

"Hey, Boot," he says. "What happened?" He looks concerned.

"Fell down the basement steps," Boot says.

"Really?" We're walking into the game room, but he's watching Boot's face carefully. I don't think he believes him.

"Yeah," Boot says.

Will Boot and I ever stop making up lies to protect our dads? I guess that's part of the game.

"And Mick signed your cast?" he says. He reads what I wrote. "And in rhyme, too!" He's mocking me, but it's funny and pretty cool.

"Well . . ." I exaggerate a modest little bow, and he laughs.

Boot and I sit on the couch, and Mr. Maddox takes the big chair.

"So." He looks at Boot, then at me. "You've had seven days in the game room. How are you getting along now?"

"Pretty well," I say. "I think Boot will agree that we've paid our debt to society."

"Very good." And then he picks up the metaphor. "So if I release you, you're ready to be productive members of society?"

"Oh, without a doubt," I say.

"Boot?"

"Yeah, sure."

"It looks as if you used the time in the game room pretty well. I'm glad you're getting along."

"Does this mean that we don't need to come here anymore?" I ask.

"I think you're ready to go back to class," he says. "So today is graduation day. Congratulations."

"Thanks," I say.

Boot smiles, and Mr. Maddox looks intently at him. "I'm

sorry I didn't get a chance to hear you play your guitar. Maybe sometime after you get your cast off, you'll bring it to school and play for me?"

He shrugs and looks at the floor. "Yeah, maybe."

"And Mick," he says, "with your interest in reading, I hope you can give us some book recommendations for our library."

"No problem. I want some recommendations, too, so I'm going to the local library this afternoon. I'll get some suggestions from one of the new volunteers. And I'm thinking of getting a volunteer job there, myself."

"Sounds good," he says.

I smile. *He has no idea how good.*

We get up, and he walks us back out to the outer office.

"Stop in once in a while at lunchtime," he says. "We'll break out the Battleship game."

"Yeah, Boot," I say. "For old time's sake."

Boot nods and says, "Cool."

"See you later." He disappears into his office.

Boot and I walk around the counter and into the hall.

"Well, I guess I don't mind going back to language arts class," I say. "Actually, it's my favorite subject."

"Nothing's *my* favorite subject," Boot says.

"So . . ." I can't think of anything to say.

"Yeah, well . . ." Apparently, he can't either.

"Okay . . ." I shrug. "Well, see you."

"Yeah, see you."

We turn and walk away in opposite directions. But I think of something.

"Hey, Boot," I call out.

He stops and turns back to me.

I fish a package of Life Savers from my pocket and toss it to him. He catches it.

"A whole roll of cherry," I tell him. "My favorite. Graduation present from the game room."

Boot smiles. He slides the candy into his pocket, then takes out the lighter and throws it to me.

I actually catch it. "But I don't smoke," I tell him.

He shrugs. "It's so you won't get caught in the dark. It'll scare the mice away."

I laugh and give him a salute.

He holds up his good hand in a little wave. We turn again and head off to our own classrooms.